♥ **The best of lig**
girls who love t

JEANETTE WINTERSON

Librarian Beatrice Hawksworth is contented with her life. True, not much happens in the sleepy New Forest town where she lives with her mother, Maisie. Much-loved Maisie whose grip on reality is fading fast, but whose flashes of insight recall the woman she once was.

Then into their lives, like a breath of fresh air, comes Harriet, escaping London, escaping Maggie with her demands and her philandering. Harriet, so sure of who she is; so safe in her sexuality.

Slowly at first, then with increasing fear – and excitement – Beatrice is forced to take stock of her past in order to find the courage to start living her present in a way that is true to her deepest self.

A moving and passionate debut novel from an exciting new lesbian talent.

"A moving study of loves laboured and lost"
EMMA DONOGHUE

JANE
THOMPSON

Still
Crazy

First published in Great Britain 1994 by
Silver Moon Books, 68 Charing Cross Road,
London WC2H 0BB

Phototypeset by Intype, London

Printed in Great Britain by
The Guernsey Press Co. Ltd, Guernsey, C.I.

ISBN 1 872642 209

A CIP catalogue record for this title is available from
the British Library

Silver Moon Books, London
and Silver Moon Books of Leeds
are in no way connected

JANE THOMPSON

Still Crazy

Prologue

It was one of those sharp and piercing November days. The sky a clear blue wash. The sun anxious to disappear into another hemisphere. Another season. The first thick frost of winter clouding the forest in white; the sun faded and irresolute, taking hours to chip through to the dank, soft earth beneath. Beatrice had spent her usual wakeful night. Unable by any means to shift the thought of Harriet from her mind. No word for days and she was feeling abandoned.

Harriet's frequent bouts of silence had the capacity to crumple her like a spent carton. Though she was unaware of how completely she had pre-occupied Beatrice's mind, the smallness of her world the restrictions, the boundaries of her life. Oblivious to how immense the place she now occupied had become.

Beatrice passed the station on her way to work. A simple unassuming country place. Needing a coat of paint. Unhurried by the usual excess of coming and going. But yet it haunted her dreams. The times Harriet had left her to go to Maggie. The once or twice she'd phoned her from the call box, wanting her. Occasionally demanding that she come. But usually it was the place from which she left.

Beatrice saw Harriet's yellow beetle parked unsteadily by the wall, as if in a rush. She'd gone again on a day she might have called. Perhaps she'd phone to see how Beatrice was. How quickly disappointment shifts desire into a new craving, to be anticipated, longed for, measured against the ticking of the clock as time runs out. She didn't, of course. And another day slipped by.

Beatrice

The alarm rang at seven. As usual it was unnecessary. Beatrice was already awake. But it was a ritual she couldn't relinquish. One of the routine procedures that gave shape to her day.

She slept only fitfully. The winter darkness slow to brighten into daylight. She had been wide awake since four, the imponderables that pre-occupied her thoughts rushing in immediately to take root in their usual positions. At least she could snuggle in the warm space beneath the covers for some little while longer. More time to shelter from the world. Except that her bed was not a friend these days. Razor blades cut through the mattress. The pillows roughly hewn rocks. The sheets twisted like tendrils of a vine, tying her in knots. It felt, she imagined, like a theatre of war, in which she tossed and struggled in solitude, to fight off the monsters that battered at the door, that filled her dreams with fear.

By seven she was glad to get up. At least the world had tasks to divert her. Work to be done. Responsibilities to be taken into account. As usual she could step back from despair as the routine of her day moved in to claim her attention. Maisie was already banging on the bedroom door.

'Bea I want my dinner. Let me out. Bea where are you? Is it dinner time?'

'I'm coming Maisie'.

She couldn't seem to call her Mother any more. So much like a child had she become. So totally had their roles been swapped. Now Beatrice was the one in charge. The one who provided food and comfort. The one who must be patient. She unlocked the door.

'You're up early Maisie. Did you sleep well? Put your dressing gown on, my Sweet, so's you don't get cold.'

'It's gone', said Maisie defiantly. 'I don't see it. Someone's taken it.'

The old lady looked tiny and frail. Her wispy grey hair was pushed under a woolly hat. White skinny arms stuck out of her nightdress like sticks. She'd spilt something tacky down the front. Her feet were crushed into battered elderly slippers, the wrong way round.

'Look it's here', said Beatrice, retrieving it from the floor. 'Let me help you put it on before you catch cold. Let's sort these slippers shall we? Look they're on the wrong feet.'

Maisie examined her feet in confusion, shaking her

head as if the effort to concentrate on the problem was beyond her.

'I might go to Newcastle', she said. 'Go and see Agnes.'

'Agnes doesn't live there anymore, Maisie. Why don't you go downstairs and put the kettle on?'

'You don't know where Agnes lives. I know. I'm writing to say I'll come.'

'You do that, Sweetie. But could you put the kettle on first?'

Agnes of course had been dead for ten years. Maisie planned to visit her friend two or three times a week, but she'd usually forgotten about it by the time she got downstairs.

Bea had a quick shower and chose a clean shirt and a cardigan. Something warm. The library was cold this time of year. Once she had made breakfast and washed the dishes and cajoled Maisie into dressing, it was half past eight. It would be much quicker to spoon the porridge into Maisie's mouth herself and put her into her clothes. And maybe it would come to that. But she resisted in the vain hope that preserving Maisie's frail grasp on responsibility would delay the creeping senility that was taking over her mind and blotting out her memory.

At the same time every morning the minibus arrived to take Maisie to the day centre. Bea waved from the doorstep to a blank frightened face at the bus window, her heart catching in sadness, as it always did, as she watched her tiny, once resilient mother, being whisked away. She took her coat and handbag from the hall stand and set off for work.

As she drove past the station she saw that Harriet's beetle was gone from the car park. Looking to check, twice daily as she went in and out to work, had become another of her rituals. If the car was there it meant she was in London struggling with Maggie. No car at the station meant Harriet was at home in the Forest. This information always cheered her up. She liked to feel that Harriet was at least somewhere close by. It also raised her expectations that she might telephone, or call at the library to change her books. She would try not to dwell too hopefully on the possibility to avert disappointment. But her wishes and desires had a mind of their own.

Quite often she wondered how they were in bed together.

Harriet said they didn't make love much any more. But did they rub shoulders? Did they lie in each other's arms? Did they read and tell about their dreams? Harriet said that once, when Maggie couldn't sleep, she'd read stories to soothe her until the dawn came. Bea thought of all the nights she'd lain awake, in fractured solitude, thinking of Harriet. The only other person in the house her crazy mother, locked into her room for safety, singing tuneless little arias in her sleep, her dreams as disconnected as her waking.

Mr Parkinson, the county librarian, was a temperamental man. He liked to run a tight ship. Bea often wondered if he ever read a book, so hostile did he appear to imagination and fantasy. He disapproved of almost everything from the length of the junior assistant's skirts to new fangled ideas about play activities for children. He had been accustomed to libraries being retreats of hushed silence, frequently empty, with books arranged neatly on shelves in alphabetical order, undisturbed by relentless readers. He suspected browsers of being malingerers from gainful employment, and made those who huddled over newspapers, sheltering from the cold, as uncomfortable as possible, until they felt obliged to leave.

He considered Beatrice to be like himself, a professional. One whose life, being meaningless in every other respect, should revolve around the library. He did not treat her as an equal, though. He had a strong sense of status.

Today he was in a bureaucratic mood and had decided, in his wisdom, that Local History needed to be completely re-arranged, re-organised and re-classified. Bea arrived to a list of instructions which he had drawn up, at some point in the middle of the night, when he too had nothing better to do.

'I expect this will take you most of today and tomorrow, Miss Hawksworth', he said. 'I'll release Mrs Spencer to tidy up the Record Library and Mrs Emsworth can look after Returns and Loans. Please report to me when the job is done.'

Actually the task suited Bea very well. It meant she could retreat into the Small Reference section, where if Harriet should come to do her writing, she always chose to sit. The job he had created was to construct a mountain out of a molehill. Like most men, it made him feel important to pretend that major tasks were being completed under his jurisdiction.

Today was Wednesday and on Wednesdays the library closed at two. This was the afternoon Beatrice allowed herself the luxury of afternoon tea at the Magnolia Cafe. She always took a book, feeling self conscious on her own. But she rarely read it. Mostly she listened to what people were saying at adjoining tables and observed the current state of tension between the two men who worked there. She guessed that most people would be oblivious to this, concerned only with consumption and their need to be serviced. But for Bea the men were by far the most interesting ingredients on the menu.

She could tell they were involved. Talking as if their lives depended on it, their voices often earnest, frequently flirtatious. Sometimes, when she observed that they were especially intense or amorous, they turned up the music as an illusion of privacy. She had come to associate the extravagance of Vivaldi with the intensity of life at the Magnolia Cafe.

Today something was wrong. There was tension hanging like pollution in the atmosphere. Jack was looking belligerant. Ralph was looking tense. Neither passed the other without a click of irritation, a pronounced sigh. At one point they both disappeared behind the Chinese lacquered screen that blocked off the storage space. This was where, in more lustful moods, they stole the odd swift kiss. She knew because she'd seen them. When they emerged Jack was rubbing his eyes and Ralph was snapping at a customer who had the temerity to ask for a vegetarian lasagne.

At some point the phone rang. Bea realised the exchange was significant because of the ferocity with which Ralph slammed down the receiver. She could only speculate about the substance of the day's drama. But clearly loss, jealousy and anger had a lot to do with it. She felt her life oddly drawn to those of the men. But knew, that like everyone else, they probably regarded her as the quiet spinster from the library, who fussed excessively about the strength of her Earl Grey tea and, these days, rarely smiled.

Callas was singing Puccini, the anguished prayer of Tosca, desperate to escape the unwanted advances of the hateful Baron. Jack and Ralph were arguing behind the counter, distracted from the buzz around them as if they were no longer part of it. A woman waited patiently to place her order, coughing self consciously to register her existence. Bea longed to rush into the kitchen, rehearsing in her head what she would say.

'Go now. Go to the sea. Put some space around yourselves. Sort out your problems. I'll hold the fort. Any fool can make tea and cut slices of cake.'

'I thought you might be here.' Suddenly the argument and the Cafe slipped into obscurity as the world shifted into another shade of light, leaving just the music and Harriet standing beside her.

'You made me jump', Bea said, her heart feeling as though it had stopped beating.

'Such a creature of habit', smiled Harriet. 'How are you?'

'All right', said Bea, reluctant to make herself any more vulnerable than she was already feeling. 'I'd get you some tea but there's high drama going on behind stairs. It seems insensitive to interrupt.'

Harriet knew the two men well. She cast a knowing glance towards the counter.

'Their respective minders have found out', she said. 'And suddenly multiple relationships aren't nearly so popular as they'd imagined them to be. I'll just go and serve myself. They won't even notice.'

Ralph and Jack smiled weakly in acknowledgement of Harriet's appearance and returned to their anguish.

She made Beatrice some more tea and cut a slice of carrot cake, taking another wedge for herself and a capuccino.

'It always ends in tears', she said wryly to the fraught lovers as she returned to Bea's table.

'Where have you been?' Beatrice asked, knowing Harriet didn't like to be cross examined. That her need to know about Harriet's life caused her irritation. But the words were out before she could control them.

'The usual', she said. 'Maggie was doing something on television and I agreed to hold her hand.'

'Isn't she capable of standing on her own feet?' Bea knew she sounded petulant. 'I thought she was so impressive and successful.'

'She likes me to be there', Harriet said. 'Anyway, she's not as self confident as you might think. None of us are. Look, it was no big deal, Bea. I wanted to see my sister and mother whilst I was in town. Why am I explaining all this to you?'

'I'm sorry'. Bea softened. 'It's just I think you should be doing your own work, not hers. And anyway, I missed you.'

'I missed you too.' Harriet closed her hand over Bea's where it rested on the table. She stroked her fingers gently, searching Bea's face for information.

'Don't hassle me Beatrice. I've got enough to deal with in my life just now. I can't take much more.'

She looked so little, so young and vulnerable. Bea couldn't sustain the rub of hostility she'd been rehearsing during Harriet's absence.

'Can I do anything to help?' she said. 'I could lend you money. I could cook you dinner. Are you eating properly? You look exhausted'

'Bea , I'm fine, honestly. I don't want your money. But yes, I'd like to have dinner with you sometime soon. I've got some news for you about Lotta. It's all a bit vague I'm afraid, but I think I've got a new lead.'

Bea watched the way her body leaned forward when she was excited, the sudden seriousness that came into her voice, the intense blue of her eyes, sparkling like cornflowers in a hayfield. Eyes that could cut through diamonds. So exactly like Lotta, it was uncanny. Like Lotta, caught unawares by Bea's camera on the bridge at Malham, her face full of eager youthfulness, describing some scheme she'd contrived to change her life. Caught like a sunbeam in time. Now more than twenty years on. She'd never told Harriet how much she looked like Lotta. How swiftly laughter brightened her eyes, like Lotta. The easy way in which she occupied the space in which she moved. The line along her brow that furrowed as she tussled with a problem. As she watched Harriet now across the table ,and as the darkness of the late November afternoon gathered at the doors and windows, Lotta fused in and out of focus as in a dream. And in her dreams, the light, agile body that she kissed was both Harriet and Lotta. The times she woke with the cry of coming on her lips, that left her curious and unsure about who had been her lover, it could have been either. It felt a difficult truth to tell. And so she said nothing.

'How is Maisie?' Harriet asked.

'As mad as usual' Beatrice smiled. 'She's taken to wearing her woolly hat in bed in case anyone tries to cut her hair. She wears it in the bath. I don't mind on the whole, except that now, hair washing has become a major drama.'

'Would she let me do it? We could make it into a game.'

'You could try. She likes you. I think she gets irritated

9

with my continual bickering. She'd be pleased to see you anyway.'

'Look, I'll come on Friday, Bea. Is that OK with you? I've got a few things to sort out tomorrow.'

Bea would like to have claimed six previous engagements but she had none. Would like to have magnified the significance of her daily chores into 'things to sort out' more important than seeing Harriet. But she wasn't up to playing games or trying to balance the uneasy swing of power that lay between them.

'That will be lovely. I'll make some dinner and you can try your charms on Maisie.'

'Don't be tetchy with me, Bea. All this is very difficult for me too, you know. You're very prickly when you're cross.'

'You're very beautiful.' A tear trickled down Bea's cheek.

'Stop it now' said Harriet. 'There's enough melodrama in this Cafe as it is to fuse a powder keg.'

Bea brushed the tear from her cheek. She should learn to be less obvious, she knew it. Each desperate declaration of desire drove Harriet further from her. Made her more wary. Made Bea feel more ashamed. More abandoned.

'So we'll say Friday, then. Unless you change your mind.'

'I won't change my mind', said Harriet. 'I never do. But if there's ructions at home that make things difficult. You know I'll come if I can.'

Later, on the way home, the barriers were down at the station. The 5.45 from London was pulling to a halt. As Bea passed the car park, she saw Harriet walking to the platform to wait for Maggie. What perfect timing. Three minutes sooner or five minutes later and she could

10

have avoided the stab of pain that caught her breath and spilled sharp, salty tears down her cheeks for the second time that afternoon.

On Friday Harriet phoned to say she couldn't come. When Beatrice asked why, she said,

'Look, it's difficult, that's all. I'll tell you later.'

That night Beatrice imagined that the world was full of lovers, sipping wine from each other's lips, brushing gentle fingers against skin, whispering and dancing in the dark. Eyes frivolous in the light of candles, teeth hungry against bone, thighs sticky with sweat.

So long, Beatrice thought, since she'd laid herself beside a woman. Felt the stretch of her limbs. Tasted sweetness on her tongue. Pulled her fingers through tousled hair. Counted freckles. Buried her face in pale shadowed thighs. Just when she thought the old longing had gone. That her sex had died. Her body had retreated from herself. Her mind attuned to questions of survival and practical solutions to the small significance of her life. Her lumpy body, forty five in June. So unused to making love. So neglected now by those who might have loved her. Touched carefully into light and heat and tumult only by herself. A poor substitute. Second best.

At first, when Lotta left, she used to make love still on her behalf. Except that, she cried so when she came, with such grief and desolation, she had to force Lotta from her mind. Forget the glint of mischief in her eyes. Block the imprint of Lotta's lovely soft skinned beauty from her thoughts. And become her own lover. Increasingly familiar. Less persistent with the years. Settling for comfort in place of passion. Looking for solace in solitude. Slipping into sleep. A good book. Warm night-gown. Clean, crisp sheets smelling of sandlewood. Forgetting and forgotten.

Till Harriet arrived. Like laughter after pain. Confusing her with memories of Lotta. Charging her with new emotion.

Harriet

This time last year Harriet was still in London. She was hanging by a strap to the ceiling of the tube. Clinging by her fingertips to some degree of competence. Attached only by a thread to the life she knew.

The train was crowded in the evening rush to displace work with home. Inanimate faces on top of disconnected bodies lined the seats. Some lost in other space and time. Others temporarily transported into the turbulence of fiction between lurid covers. Or drowned in the tawdry speculation of the tabloid press. The aisles and lobbies were tight with bodies, forcing unwanted contact, lurching to the swing of the train. Pressed into separate proximity. Staring but not seeing. Pushing beyond the crush of isolated people and out towards the mean, anonymous streets.

Harriet's heart began to pound. She searched the serried faces for signs of recognition. Registered the smell and heave of flesh without feeling or connection. The grind of metal on burnished tracks, the clatter of buffers and bolts that echoed to the rattle of the train. Conversation non existent. Talk reduced to fragments.

She was sweating now, afraid she couldn't breathe. The crush closing down. The walls and ceilings pressing in. No one conscious of her rising panic. Her fingers shaking on the handle of the strap, her mind holding to a memory. 'The world falls apart. The centre cannot hold.' She needed air. She needed out. 'Mind the gap.' A disembodied voice was ordering her actions. The doors rapped shut and the train plunged on. What if she were to lose control? To faint? To scream? To die? Who here would cry or care?

She struggled through the mass of bodies towards the exit, sharp tears stinging her eyes, tigers beating at her breast. No one softened. No one noticed that her body shook. That she was gasping.

The train shuddered to a standstill, the platform full of shifting blocks and dead barriers. As she reached the stair the air rushed by and felt less hostile. But it was stale and rank with dust and sweat and pee. Then she was surfacing. Soon she would see the sky and feel the bite of winter wind against her cheek.

Outside the station a band was playing carols and gaudy lights flickered from trees and garlands on tinselled shop facades and window ledges. A drunken man

14

was selling newspapers that told of Christmas on the streets in cardboard city and bombs in Northern Ireland.

A young woman in a flimsy jacket and a cotton dress, her face white with hunger and bruised with sores, was crouched beside the station wall, clutching a baby in a dirty blanket, her hand stretched out for money. Harriet stopped to touch her heart, unsure that she could stand. She breathed long and deep, opening her lungs to the taste of soot and smog, closing her eyes to ease the pounding in her brain. The woman didn't look up. Harriet couldn't look down.

She moved out across the road and through the broken, dusty streets to home. That day at school she had almost lost her nerve. A boy, waiting to be noticed, threw a chair. The books she planned to use in class arrived ripped and stencilled with obscenities. In the staff room grey faced teachers slid into corners between lessons, smoking to excess, and choosing to ignore the sounds of mayhem in the yard. Few left with any energy to spare. The Head rarely visible outside her office, except to invent meetings in other locations that required her presence.

As Harriet walked the streets that led to and from the school, she couldn't blame the children. The houses were decaying, some squatted, others boarded up. The hatred of the dispossessed was written on the crumbling walls. Rubbish piled high in concrete gardens where dust carts and itinerant milkmen no longer called. Broken cars, their wheels burned out and their insides gutted, rotted by the kerb.

The young men, menacing and brash in gangs, who whistled as she passed, were high on hopelessness and short on jobs. The women, pushing prams and buggies through doors that stuck with damp and creaked on broken hinges, were already old. Behind dank curtains and grimy windows, someone spoke of sunshine. Waiting for a parcel or a letter that might bring relief, but which never came. Abandoned like the rest by those who had the temerity or luck to leave.

Harriet knew this life too well. She'd come from streets like these in Leeds. Seen her own life change through education and a push in the right direction. Fresh out of university she wanted to make room for others. She laboured hard, trying to construct relevance and self reliance in grubby classrooms amidst grubby children. And for eight years now she walked this route to work. Watching the disintegration of the Local State. Its inability to cope. Its powers dismantled by grey suited bureaucrats in air conditioned buildings administering instructions. She watched the developers move in along the River, shaping effigies to greed and profit, smart shops and offices and flats for yuppies. Their affluence obscene against the drift to chaos and collapse. And now her energy was exhausted. Her nerve was spent.

Even at home she no longer felt safe. Once recently she'd returned to find the windows smashed and LEZZIE CUNT burned in red across the wall. She'd fixed massive bolts to the doors and drilled a spy hole to see who knocked. Increasingly she felt besieged. Flat mates came and went and quit in search of space and easier employment. Sharing with friends, the great investment in communal living, now floundered on the back of disillusion and recession. Women lost hope in politics. Burned too many bridges. Fled from argument and conflict into personal solutions for survival. Monogamy. The countryside. Babies. And therapy. Now rooms were let to 'non smokers' who answered ads in arty magazines. Without shared views or expectations or conditions in common, they passed on stairs and landings intent upon separate missions.

Harriet was growing thin and gaunt. She'd lost her appetite and enough self esteem to contemplate collapse. She stopped visiting the gym and was afraid to run the streets at night. Increasingly she lived on bread and cheese and marmalade. A glass of whisky to unwind. Red wine to cheer her up. Brandy to help her sleep. On top of everything, she knew that Maggie was lying to her again – this time in New Orleans.

For three days she stayed in bed, unable to persuade herself with reason, or arguments about responsibility, to face the world. She lay for hours watching where a butterfly, its wings wrapped against flight, clung to the fold of the cornice. She considered whether it was dead or merely sleeping. And how it came to winter in her room. She'd thought that for butterflies, life was brilliant but brief, a squandering of passion amidst summer flowers. The question defeated her.

She drifted in and out of sleep and knew that part of her anxiety was exhaustion. On Thursday Maggie telephoned from New Orleans sounding tipsy. She was at a publishing convention, trading books and signing authors. Her favourite excuse for licence and largesse. Harriet knew she'd taken Sophie. She also knew she must sound boring and jealous by comparison, but found it difficult to be enthusiastic about the prospect of Maggie rampant and unrepressed.

'How's the blackboard jungle?' Maggie shouted down the phone before the line went dead.

'I could be buried alive for all you'd care.' Harriet pulled the covers around her head and cried.

By Friday she knew she needed help, much as it went against her nature to admit it. She rang her sister, conscious that one more wave and she would drown.

'Hold tight', Helen said at once. 'I'm coming over. Get up and wash your face and pack your bag. You're coming to spend Christmas here with me'.

When she thought about it later she knew she'd seen the edge of breaking. And somethings in her life now had to change. It was time to face defeat and start again.

'You've served your time', Helen said. 'No one could accuse you of not trying. And there are lots of kids who'll know you made a difference. Who are stronger in themselves because of you. Now you owe it to yourself to make a break. Find some space in which to breathe. Some peace and quiet. It's no big deal to quit, you know. Your sanity is what's at stake.'

London felt hostile. A sprawling ugly monster on the loose. Brutal and intent upon revenge. Harriet yearned for gentleness, a lightness to her day.

'You could try the country for a while', Helen said. 'Somewhere fresh to start again. Where nothing happens very much. Time to think.'

Maggie didn't want Harriet to leave town. She liked her own independence, of course. To pretend that she was unattached. But she liked to know that Harriet was around, preferably fully occupied. Dedicated. Safe.

When she came back from New Orleans she was guilty and contrite as usual. Her infidelity predictable but ephemeral. Her interest was always in the chase, the

18

conquest. She had limited powers of concentration. She always came back. Lying to conceal her lies. Attentive with phone calls and flowers and tickets for the opera.

Helen hated Maggie. She was the only person Harriet knew who was totally unimpressed by Maggie's powerful job in publishing, her smart flat in Hampstead, her gregarious confidence that swept women off their feet. Like all the rest Harriet had been dazzled by her charm. Intoxicated by her wit. Seduced by the tireless attention which Maggie devoted to the cultivation of a new recruit. From Harriet's bedsit on the front line, her workplace at the coal face, Maggie smelled of romance and luxury and power. And despite the rest of her acolytes, Maggie reserved some curious need for Harriet's continuing presence, so long as her own wayward promiscuity need never be the forfeit.

'What Maggie needs of course is a wife', Helen said with feeling, bitter about the way in which she carelessly squandered Harriet's emotions and abused her loyalty.

'I'm surprised you put up with it. You're not a doormat in any other respect.'

Harriet couldn't be objective. There were times, like now, when she also knew she'd had enough. But there was another side to Maggie. A shyness rarely seen. A need to be nurtured. A fear of failure. A distaste about herself that was touched with madness. The kind of weakness that only Harriet knew. When she was feeling sorry for her, she couldn't leave. When she was feeling impressed she liked her style. The deceit of course was something else. Easy to dismiss as the morality of a shit. Except the vanity that gave rise to her affairs was a complicated response to vulnerability. Some deep-seated damage that Harriet only partly understood. A weakness that was fed by an addiction.

It was part of Harriet's nature to struggle with complexity. To pick away at feelings and sub-conscious ways of being until they revealed meaning. She was bad at letting go. It took months of feeling drowned under water and thrown up ship wrecked on the other side of collapse to contemplate leaving the city. Leaving Maggie for reasons that were shot through with streaks of masochism was proving even more distressing.

At first, of course, it was all very different. She had met Maggie beside water.

'Do you care about the sea?' Maggie had asked, as they watched where black folds of angry waves crashed in around the cliffs beneath their feet. Where gulls swirled against the currents of wild air and dived to protect their nests from dangerous invasion. Below was limestone, licked smooth by the relentless smash of water against rock. Creased and cut along the fault line like a pavement set in ancient slabs.

'A dancing ledge', Maggie had said. 'We can dance along the ledge until the water laps around our ankles. Down there, below the stretch of thrift and lichen, there's samphire and rock pools.'

They had climbed down the jagged cliff path towards the sea. Soon out of sight, they found the makeshift steps cut by centuries into the rock face. A rough, slippery descent to a flat ledge circled now by cliffs. The battering of the waves echoed across the bay as in an ancient arena, performing against an empty sky, the gulls shrieking their applause.

At first Harriet had thought that Maggie's look of recognition was as innocent, as unexpected, as her own.

That she had held Harriet's eyes and been drawn into the rush of desire with the same tremble of surprise. But later she knew she'd been consciously seduced. That Maggie knew about such things. About smouldering looks. About the fleeting brush of fingers against flesh. About focusing her attention with precision, until the object of her lust became expansive and easy in the excitement of being wanted. Harriet, like all the rest, had been delighted to be teased and bullied into bed. It had been a game in which she felt no anguish. Just the slightest chill of fear. Knowing this was not a woman to be resisted.

And at first Maggie was a dedicated lover.

'Come just as you are.' She tumbled Harriet into bed, her white linen shirt unloosed at the collar. Her jeans unbuttoned at the waist.

'Leave your clothes to me. I like undoing women.'

Harriet waited until her shirt fell open under practised, determined fingers, her cunt already aching before Maggie slipped beneath the silk and pulled away her pants.

'Now. Now.' She had never pleaded like this before.

Later she watched Maggie go, tall and striding at the door, disappearing. She wanted to call out. Call her back. Feel the twist of her fingers on the hair at the back of her neck. The pressure of Maggie's grip on her breast that made her cry out. She was beautiful this tall and striding woman. Already moving to her own rhythm.

Those were the days when love was sharp and sweet upon Harriet's tongue and her body smelled of sex.

'I write to a woman in Woodleigh', Helen said, 'who

21

might know about cottages to rent in the New Forest. Would that appeal to you?'

'It would be wonderful', Harriet said. 'I could try out the book I've always wanted to write. Live on my savings for a while. Get little bits of work to keep me going.'

'You could do some private coaching if you didn't want to teach full time.'

'Yes. Or help with the harvest. Pick strawberries. Make tea for the tourists. I don't mind. Tell me about your friend.'

'She's called Beatrice Hawksworth. She works at the library at Winslow. I've never met her personally, but I feel I know her well. Meeting might feel quite strange after all this time. We've both resisted it. After everything we've said in letters.'

Harriet was intrigued. 'How did you start writing?'

'I answered an ad in a contact magazine for lesbian pen friends. That probably sounds pathetic to you. But I was tired of world-weary London dykes, so busy being jaded and critical of each other. And quite suddenly everyone looked seventeen or like a storm trooper'.

'Is Beatrice lesbian then?'

'Yes. But fairly isolated I would say. Winslow is a long way from London, you know. It's the sticks down there.'

'In the closet, you mean?'

'I think she's probably so far into the closet that she can't remember where she hid the closet. I think you'd like her, though. She's very intense and has an amazing past, if she ever gets round to telling you about it'.

'What's that?'

'Oh that's for Bea to say. It might be a secret. Sometimes you say things in letters, when you imagine you're never going to meet, that you don't admit to easily in other contexts. I'm very furtive, as you know, but I've written things to Bea that I've never said to anyone else, even lovers.'

'You didn't tell me you had a pen friend. I thought those organisations were a veiled excuse for sex.'

'You didn't ask me', Helen laughed. 'Too intent about reconstructing the ghetto and being tossed about by Maggie's turbulent demands.'

'Two dykes in one family. It's not a bad score is it?' Harriet laughed. 'I blame the midwife.'

'I thought you attributed your choice to solidarity', Helen teased. 'You told me you could no longer think of sleeping with the enemy. As a matter of principle. And when you get the hots for Maggie, I suppose that's a political statement is it?'

'Well I used to get the hots for men too when I was young and foolish. And I suppose it seemed all right at the time.'

'How could you sleep with all those dreadful men in the History department? I never understood it. One of them was old enough to be your grandfather.'

'A slight exaggeration on your part, Helen. He wasn't that old, he just looked old. Something to do with being the professor. It was power I suppose. I thought they had power and I wanted some of it. That, and flattery. The attention they paid me made me feel significant.'

'How young and stupid can you be', said Helen. 'Except, when it comes to you and Maggie, those dreadful cliches still probably apply.'

'It's much more complicated now', Harriet said defensively.

'It would be', Helen sighed, anxious to change the subject before she got really irritated. 'What you need is fun. A holiday. A little untroubled romance in your life. And to hell with Maggie. Come on now. Write your let-

ters. One to resign from the coal face and one to ask
Bea about cottages to rent and what news she has from
nowhere.'

Lotta

Her lover lay buried in sleep, oblivious to the crash of waves against the sea wall. The woman watched wide-eyed as the dawn lifted lightness into the shadows of the room. Four in the morning was a bad time to be alone with memories of her former life.

'This makes it all worthwhile', she thought.

A sheepskin rug was thrown across the dark brown knotted floorboard, scrubbed and polished down the years by more industrious wives. A baby lay on her back, tiny fists and feet pushing and kicking at the air, in a minute struggle to be standing. The sunshine, cut and sliced into shafts of dusty light by the leaded windows, streaked across the room, pricking spots of orange and green along the shadows on the wall. The baby watched where the sunlight flickered, reaching to catch the illusive jewels in her tiny fingers. She gurgled and blew noisy bubbles.

'Raspberries' her mother called them, as she wiped the crumbs from the breakfast table and piled marigolds and mombretia into a brown, terracotta vase. She watched the baby as she worked, her dark wispy head buried in the tangled woollen skin of the animal. She looked for some likeness in the child to herself but she could see none.

'She's mine, though, this one. She makes the rest worthwhile. Time to play now', the woman cooed, lifting the baby into her arms and wrapping her in a soft green knitted shawl to keep warm. 'Let's go and see the ducks.'

She carried the child across the yard and beside the low stone wall to the orchard. Chickens and ducks squabbled noisily in search of grain; the hens picking through the spiky grass with nervous persistence. The baby watched with rapt attention, her arms freeing themselves from the folds of the shawl to catch the leaves on the apple trees. The woman sang as she carried the child to the gate and across the meadow, dappled with poppies, to the stream.

'Suzanne takes you down
to her place by the river.
You can watch the boats go by.
You can spend the night beside her . . .'

It was a gentle landscape, soft green, gold and warm

26

sienna. Wide and tumbling towards the flatness of the valley beyond. The corn was good this year. Just enough wetness to swell the grain. Plenty of sun to turn the sharp, green spears fat and golden. In the distance she could hear the shout of men working in the fields, their machines beginning to gather home the harvest. The woman had no desire to take the baby closer. She would learn these things soon enough.

The village was the place to be. Grey-stoned cottages snaked around a pond and along a stream towards the high street. It was unremarkable enough to remain a working village. The schoolmistress had moved in from Manchester eight years earlier but almost everyone else was local born and bred.

The woman felt like an outsider. Village life was curious and sharp with gossip, but the baby helped to ease her way into its heart; the women's guild, the playgroup and the village hall. She got to know the shopkeepers and was often called in for coffee at the vicarage as she passed by with her pram. Few women can resist new babies, and their possession lends at least an illusion of respectability. But the woman knew that her arrival had not passed without comment.

Her husband owned a moderate-sized farm on the fringes of the village and was considered eligible but unlikely. He was thirty-five when she married him and had seemed, to those who noticed such things, to be a determined bachelor. The baby appeared soon after.

'Too soon', some said with a knowing look.

'I never imagined the sexual revolution would reach Roe Appleby', Mrs Pratt had told the vicar's wife who told the schoolmistress.

But the woman was keen to please. To be accepted. This was her life now. Whatever else she may have wanted, she had the baby to consider, and to love. The baby would make the rest worthwhile.

In the winter she joined a painting class in the village hall. It was attended mostly by young wives, like herself, and they took it in turns to mind the children. It was a good excuse to be with women. They talked and laughed as much as they painted. Once, Beryl Scott agreed to pose in the nude for the life class, and during the summer months they stopped copying from postcards and women's magazines and took their paints and easels into the countryside. Beryl Scott always insisted on a picnic and began the tradition of including a bottle or two of Blue Nun.

'Its very artistic', she said.

Mrs Pratt and the vicar's wife quite liked to talk about their husbands but no one else was very much interested. Marriage, it seemed, was a necessary evil. Its what they did because they had to. Everybody did. They wanted children, they got married. They endured the consequences in private. In the evenings when the men came home from work. On Sunday when the in-laws came for lunch. On Saturday night at the Farmers' Social Club. But the rest of the time men were irrelevant. They went to work. The women looked after the children. And rushed through the housework to meet friends for coffee in the village, catch up with the news at the playgroup, go on painting expeditions with the art class. None of it of any interest to the men. Women's stuff, women's lives; hobbies, gossip, kids: designed to keep them happy.

The woman's husband usually came home at seven, just as she was putting the baby to bed. She watched as he directed a rough, weathered hand towards the baby's chin.

'Chuck. Chuck. Chuck.' he said as he stroked the pink dimples momentarily. 'Who's Daddy's pretty little girl?'

The woman waited, slightly irritated. He was a man of few words.

'Will you wash yourself before supper?' She asked as usual.

He strode into the bathroom and the woman put the baby down to sleep. After supper the man went to the pub or to the Farmers' Union meeting. His hair was thinning at the front, she noticed, his stomach was spreading beneath his comfortable cord trousers.

She lit the oil lamp by the fire and opened the door slightly, in case the baby should wake up. From the box in the pine dresser she took out her collection of records and maps and laid them on the table. She wanted to check whether the Grand Canyon was in California or Arizona. It was probably of no account but it felt important to be certain.

On the Dancette in the corner 'Eleanor Rigby swept up the leaves from the church where the wedding had been. Lived in a dream . . .'

For several years she lived like this. She among the women. He among the men. But things were getting more difficult.

'Can't you keep them quiet?' The farmer had lost money on some pigs and came home in a foul temper. His family had multiplied. The woman could remember precisely the moment when the seeds were sprouted. Sex was by then a rare event. Years of celibacy before he met her made the man undemanding. And the woman unimpressed. Although occasionally she had no option. Once, after a trip to the city with his friends, he returned in an agitated mood. He pressed her greedily against the bed, his breath smelling of tobacco and whisky. That was Hal.

Andrew was conceived as the light faded on St David's Day. It was the time Caroline had come with daffodils and leeks and they made posters for the women's festival in York. As the children hurtled around the garden and chased chickens through the orchard, Caroline pulled her fingers through the woman's curls and traced the line of her breast beneath her cotton shirt.

The man came home sooner than they expected. Crashing into the tiny kitchen where the two women and their children were eating jelly and telling stories. The room a disaster zone. The children's laughter and excitement suddenly contagious. He appeared like a martian at a garden fete. Alien, obtrusive, disturbing. The women blushed. The children abruptly silent, unsure what to do.

Later that evening he took the woman quickly and with little grace. She stared at the ceiling where a spider struggled in the web it had previously spun for itself. And she cried in pain as he pushed into her body, releasing tears from her eyelids like a burst of hailstones. That was Andrew.

'I'm sorry if your deal fell through', she said, 'But its not the children's fault.'

Upstairs the boys were shooting toy rifles at each other. The girl was practising the violin.

'If you were a proper wife . . . a decent mother . . . you would . . .' The now familiar complaints came thick and fast, hurled like handgrenades against her defences. Multiplying the confusion and doubts she could no longer keep at bay. She went into the kitchen and began making supper. But he was reluctant to let go.

'And what did you do today, may I ask? What contribution did you make to the family finances? How much did you squander on yourself? Painting and modelling and picking flowers. This is Yorkshire. 1974. You know. Not bloody Bloomsbury.'

The woman crushed garlic against the wooden salad bowl and tried to stay calm.

'Why don't you take your shower? Supper won't be long. I'll put the kids to bed before we eat.'

'And have you seen Caroline today?' He was not going to be distracted.

In fact they had made love in the orchard, beneath the apple tree.

'I expect she was here, poking her nose into my family. Playing silly bugger games with my children. Those boys need a haircut. They look like pansies.'

'Look. If you want to have a civilised discussion about my life and my friends and how I look after our children, I'm happy to talk about it. But don't come home like the heavy handed bully, screaming your bad temper at me. What's all the sudden fuss? You've shown precious little interest in us until now. I don't complain about your friends, though God knows, they're stupid enough.'

He crashed the door into the frame, blocking her escape.

'I don't want that woman here in my house again. Do you understand? I don't want her near my children. I don't want you seeing her. Do I make myself clear?'

The woman felt afraid. She backed against the wall, her body shaking, her heart thumping in her chest. She couldn't meet his eyes.

'Let me come past', she said. 'I think I can hear Andrew crying. Please let me past.'

The man grabbed her arm, his rough, weathered hands cruel on her skin. His face angry and upset.

'Just forget about her. Do you understand? Your place is here with me and the children. You can have anything you want so long as you do what's right. One step out of line and it's curtains.'

Andrew was banging on the kitchen door.

'Mummy. Mummy. Hal's hitting me with his rifle. Let me in. Let me in.'

The man pulled back, opening the door to his son. Andrew ran to the woman and buried his head in her legs sobbing uncontrollably. She lifted the child into her arms, soothing his tears amidst her own.

'Andrew for God's sake grow up', the man shouted at the toddler, 'and stop all this noise. Hal switch that bloody television off and go to bed.' The man banged upstairs to take his shower.

The next day the woman took the girl to school and the boys to playgroup and went to see Caroline. She rarely went to Caroline's house. It was in the middle of the village and her husband's shop was next door. Some days she helped him serve the customers. The woman went to say that everything was over. She couldn't go on. They sat in the small, dark room at the back of the house that overlooked the abattoir, and watched the vans unload the animals. The thought of the butcher's hands on Caroline's flesh made the woman sick.

'I've got to get out', she said. 'He'll kill me if I stay.'

'Don't tell him', Caroline said. 'He'll never guess. He's not interested in your life, not really'.

'He knows already. You don't understand. I can't pretend any longer. Its not the first time this has happened.'

'I want you to stay. I love you.'

'Then come with me.'

'You're crazy . . .'

Back beside the sea the gulls shrieked. Downstairs the clock chimed eight and the woman decided to face the new day.

'Did you have bad dreams again?' Her lover ran careful fingers along the crease of her brow.

'Old scars', she said, 'still bleeding.'

Beatrice

Beatrice was recovering from a visit to the supermarket with Maisie when Harriet's letter arrived. She didn't like to leave her on her own and thought that the longer Maisie could be encouraged to share the chores of their life together, the longer she might keep the demons in her mind at bay. But it was one of the occasions when Bea had to concede that another point of contact had been lost. In the event, she was lucky to escape without a summons.

Maisie was in a giddy mood after a week in which the day centre was closed for Christmas and she only had Bea for company. She liked Spillers. It was the biggest and brightest of the local supermarkets. It had the speediest trolleys in town and plenty of odd spaces in which to slip out of sight. Bea let her take a trolley and gave her careful instructions about what to put in it. A task she could still do, if somewhat slowly, as little as three weeks earlier. Whether it was her mood, or another symptom of her deterioration, Bea wasn't sure. But in either case, the result was pandemonium. By the time she'd slipped through Bea's fingers like Scotch mist, and found her way to the fruit and vegetable display, she was intent upon feeding an army. She piled oranges and carrots and bananas and potatoes into the trolley without stopping. It was three quarters full of assorted goodies before anyone thought to alert the staff. A man in a white uniform put a restraining hand on her sleeve, his voice less than sympathetic.

'Just a minute, Madam. You need to be putting those in small plastic bags and weighing them if your intention is to make a purchase.'

Even someone who was fully *compos mentis* would have had difficulty deciphering his pomposity. Maisie scowled, taking an immediate dislike to the colour of his overall and the grip of his fingers on her arm. She sensed anger and restriction and like a baited badger, her instinct was to flee.

Already her grasp on the concepts of normal conversation had faltered. She understood what was being said, but she could no longer fit the words she needed to reply into coherent sentences. And unless you knew her very well, and were adept at lateral thinking, her train of association was tenuous in the extreme.

'It's a problem of coming out before I go to get enough for Bea and Agnes', she shouted at the man. 'We were rationed in the war. I need to keep the pantry full in case. You should be shut up with that coat on. Don't try to stop me here. I'm off.'

But she was reluctant to leave without the trolley, convinced the provisions she was collecting were vital to her requirements. Fortunately for Maisie, Mrs Emsworth from the library was there to intervene.

'Hello Maisie dear', she said gently. 'Are you helping Beatrice with the shopping?' She gave the man the kind of look that said 'Leave this to me. Can't you see she's dotty?'

Maisie looked confused, trying to remember where she'd seen this woman before. Was it the day centre? She couldn't be sure.

'I might be.' Her response was vague, her tone emphatic.

'Is Beatrice waiting for you to bring the trolley?' Mrs Emsworth tried again.

'Maybe she is.' Maisie crossed her arms defiantly, like she was being challenged to give out information she stubbornly refused to concede.

'Shall we go and look for her? We can let this man look after the trolley till we find Beatrice.'

By now Maisie had forgotten how adamant she felt about not relinquishing the green groceries. Remembering instead that she was supposed to get marmalade and chocolate biscuits. She looked at Mrs Emsworth as if she could see right through her, oblivious to the detail of what she was saying. She turned in her tracks and scurried round the corner, past the deli and down towards the checkout. By now she had no trolley and the task of picking jars and packets off shelves, without anywhere to put them, was a difficulty which assumed enormous proportions. Her hands were shaking as she struggled to balance the items against her meagre body, whilst reaching out to add to her collection.

Suddenly it was all too troublesome. Her co-ordination snapped. She dropped her arms and the clutch of pots and packages fell smashing to the floor. Maisie was now feeling agitated. She didn't like the crash that splattered glass and sticky red jam all round her feet. She tried to kick the mess away, tears of frustration streaming down her cheeks. Everything smashed and still no marmalade and biscuits as requested. She stuffed a jar in the pocket of her coat and some biscuits in the other just as the man in the white uniform was heading in her direction.

'Bea.a.a.a.' Maisie screeched.

By now the supermarket felt a frightening place to be in, with things jumping at her from shelves, and red-faced, angry people bearing down at her from all sides. And whilst her instinct was to run, her feet felt blocked in concrete, as in a nightmare. A crowd was gathering curious in a voyeuristic way, but slow to respond to Maisie's obvious distress.

'Bea..Bea.a.a.a.' she shouted through her tears. Loud enough this time to bring Bea rushing from the other side of the store where she'd been thoughtfully selecting wine and momentarily forgetting Maisie.

'Oh Sweetheart', she said, taking her mother into her arms and hugging her close until the tears and shaking subsided. 'What a mess you're in. Was it all too much?'

Maisie looked totally defeated as if some enormous boot had stamped on her from a great height.

'Home now, Bea.' she said. 'I want to go home now.'

Bea looked towards the man in the white coat.

'Look I'm dreadfully sorry', she said. 'As you can see,

my poor mother isn't well. I'm sorry about the damage. Can you tell me how much it is? I'll be glad to pay.'

The man started to count the cost in a way that suggested he was going to make a meal of it.

'I'm sorry to be difficult', Bea said. ' But I really think I need to get my mother home. She's clearly very upset and frightened now. Can I leave you an address?'

'For God's sake. Let them go.' A woman in the crowd turned on the man. ' A few broken biscuits and the odd pot of jam isn't going to break the bank. One day this could be your mother. This could be you.'

The man was losing control.

'All right Madam', he said. 'We'll forget about it this time. I'm sorry about the old lady. But don't bring her shopping here again.'

Somewhere in the supermarket was an abandoned trolley full of fruit and vegetables. And in another corner, the weekly shop Bea had been hoping to take with her through the checkout. Two hours after setting out, they arrived home, with nothing but a lot of upset and a pot of marmalade and a packet of biscuits retrieved from Maisie's pockets.

'Put the kettle on Maisie.' Bea was exhausted. 'Would you like a chocolate biscuit with your tea?'

Bea read Harriet's letter with some excitement. The prospect of another lesbian in town, with whom she might make friends, was well worth looking forward to. She felt so isolated with only her pen friends and her memories for company. She'd begun to wonder whether 'being different to everyone else' mattered anymore. It didn't stop her feeling lonely. In lots of ways it made her feel more lonely. Not that anyone knew. In the library, customers came and went. She got to know a few. Discovered their tastes in books. Pointed out new titles. Shared the time of day. But local gossip and friends she could rely on, passed her by.

A new librarian was appointed in the summer. Mr Parkinson. She'd applied for the job herself, having worked in the service for almost thirteen years. But she didn't get it. Mr Parkinson moved down from Birmingham. His wife had recently died and he wanted a fresh start, he said.

He was a cautious, irritable little man. In fact, he was quite boring. She'd hoped he'd be a 'new broom', a 'breath of fresh air'. That, at least, might have made her own rejection bearable. She'd been on courses and was a regular correspondent to the staff magazine. She had all kinds of ideas about innovations. But she'd been given no encouragement by her previous boss and Mr Parkinson, unfortunately, was cast from the same mould.

Just before Christmas he surprised her, however.

'Miss Hawksworth, I wonder if you would care to join me for a drink and a bite to eat after work on Friday? To celebrate Christmas and our first six, happy months together.'

No one asked Beatrice to go out in the evening. She couldn't remember the last time it happened. It was difficult to find someone to sit with Maisie, but she decided to accept. If only as an act of desperation.

They went to the King's Head in the Square. Beatrice had no idea what she'd find to say to Mr Parkinson. He wasn't even much of a reader as far as she could tell. And there was a limit to what more could be said about re-classifying Large Print Fiction. He was very attentive, however. And unusually generous. She'd come to think of him as a skinflint.

On an empty stomach, the wine went straight to her head. The food, when it arrived, was good, although she would have preferred to eat fish. But as the Christmas lights dazzled on the tree, and the buzz of conversation swam around her, she felt her spirits mellow, and the tension in her shoulders slip away. As she looked around the room she watched what normal people did at festive times. Meet up with lovers and family and friends and appear, at least in public, to be happy. She was grateful not to be on her own, even if the company was only Mr Parkinson.

He was talking about how much he missed his wife. Bea was hoping Maisie was behaving herself and concentrating on the conversation at the table by the window. She watched the two women with interest. They certainly had a lot to say to each other. She watched how intensely they looked into each other's eyes and knew she wasn't alone.

Mr Parkinson was clearing his throat and ordering a second jug of wine. She knew her face was flushed and her heart was racing. But she didn't realise that he would consider this to be significant. Suddenly his hand was resting beside hers. She tried to draw back but he was obviously working himself up to a previously prepared speech. Could this be the twentieth century? She felt like a character in a Victorian melodrama.

'I am sorry if I presume, Miss Hawksworth', Mr Parkinson cleared his throat again. 'But I have been watching you for some weeks. I know you have a worrying time with your poor, dear mother, and that she occupies a lot of your attention. But you seem to me to have given up on the possibility of happiness for yourself. I too am lonely since Dorothy died and have no wish to return each evening to an empty flat. I wonder whether we could begin to spend more time together? I'm sure we'd get on famously. And who knows ... we may have more in common than just our joint commitment to the service.'

Bea wanted to laugh. But instead tears trickled down her cheeks. A signal it wasn't altogether surprising that he should mistake for sentiment and gratitude. Men are like that.

'Dear Miss Hawksworth. May I call you Beatrice? I thought I might be right.' He leant forward, taking her hand in his. She saw the women by the window get up to leave. She guessed they were going somewhere to make love. She felt her body dissolve, an echo of distant laughter stirred her memory, the thud as the door burst open and the light snapped on ...

Mr Parkinson was saying something about Christmas dinner. Was she intending to be alone or ...? Bea thought she'd better put an end to all this before she was too drunk to be coherent.

'Maisie and I will have our Christmas dinner on our own as usual thank you. It's the way we like it. We usually play charades and dominoes and Maisie sings me 'Danny Boy' as she did when I was a child. I'm grateful for your offer of friendship, and I hope we can be friends, at work as well. But I am not interested in romance, Mr Parkinson, if that is what you have in mind.' She took a swig of wine, quite amazed at her own assertion. She was tempted to continue, 'You see, I'm not like other women, I'm a lesbian.' But she lost her nerve, and after so long on her own, she wasn't even sure that it was true anymore. Instead she said, 'So thank you for your kindness. I've really enjoyed the meal. Now I think

41

I must be getting back to mother. It's almost past her bedtime.'

Although her response was extremely gentle and restrained, it was, of course, not what Mr Parkinson wanted to hear. Already the settling of the bill seemed excessive to him and like a total waste of money. He was surprised that she should consider she had a choice. Most women in her position, and at her time of life, would be only too glad to . . .

'I'll just get the barmaid to order me a taxi', she interrupted his irritation. 'No need to bother with a lift. Do you think you're in a fit state to drive Mr Parkinson?'

That was a week ago. She hadn't seen him since and hoped that the Christmas holiday had given him chance to cool down. Beatrice re-read the letter from Helen's sister. She spoke of feeling 'burned out' and 'needing to get her head together'. Neither of these were phrases that meant much to Beatrice. She imagined she was one of those immensely trendy London dykes that Helen was always joking about. She had a strangely old fashioned handwriting though, odd in the circumstances, spidery and quaint like an old lady's. Not what Bea would expect. Not much good for writing on blackboards, she thought. But she was feeling quite intrigued. She decided not to reply until she'd found somewhere that might suit. She wanted to appear reliable and decisive. Though God knows why. She was only a girl after all. And Bea had enough on her hands.

The outburst at the supermarket had exhausted Maisie and she went to bed earlier than usual that night. As Bea bent to kiss her cheek, she reached up to take her hand. In a rare moment of clarity she said, 'Don't send me away yet, Bea. Not until you have to. When I'm peeing in my pants and I can't tell if it's Christmas or

Easter, that will be the time. I shan't know then and you mustn't mind.'

'Sweetheart.' The tears gathered in Bea's eyes. 'We do all right don't we? I would never send you away.'

The old lady looked wistful. 'Never is a long time Beatrice and you have your own life to lead.'

Bea knelt to rest her head on the covers beside her mother's breast. Maisie was humming a little tune as she patted Bea's hair.

'Time to sleep now', Bea said looking up. But the old lady had already closed her eyes against the day and was taking refuge in her dreams.

Harriet

Discovering Heather Hill had been a lucky coincidence. Not long after Harriet wrote to her from London, a woman came into the library to place an advertisement on the bulletin board. Her mother, whose cottage it was, had recently died, and whilst she didn't want to live in it herself, she didn't want to sell the place. She was looking for someone who would look after it and inherit the dog and tend to the garden.

'It's a bit of a problem', the woman had said, 'because Mother never wanted any changes or improvements.

Most people wouldn't want to live without hot water or a bathroom or a reliable source of electricity.'

'I know someone who's looking for a place to rent. I could ask her', Bea said.

Bea could remember every detail of the day she first met Harriet. She had come to the library on half day closing so they could go together to see the cottage. Bea took excessive care with her clothes that day. She didn't know why. She changed two or three times before she was happy with how she looked. But the subtlety of her achievement was all in her mind. Mr Parkinson didn't notice that she looked any different. Mrs Emsworth and Mrs Spencer failed miserably to comment.

Maisie said, 'Are you going dancing Beatrice?' Which might, or might not, have registered significance.

All morning her heart felt fluttery, and a little knot of anticipation gathered tenaciously in her stomach. Each time the door swung open she looked up expectantly, even though she knew that Harriet wasn't due until closing time. She watched herself in the glass as she passed the Record Section, conscious, as never before, about the greyness of her hair, the serious set of her mouth, the frown across her eyes. She brushed her hair two or three times, trying to induce her fringe to separate and stick up so that it looked less severe and boring. She resolved to see the hairdresser and ask about highlights.

She practised being animated with the customers so that by the time Harriet arrived she would be in a more gregarious mood than had become usual. She was expecting Harriet to be street wise and worldly, and wondered why on earth she'd imagined she might like to live with no hot water or inside toilet. Helen had said she was wildly impractical, and was totally unused to living anywhere without all-night cinemas, take away kebabs, and the grind and throb of the city outside her window. But there was something about Heather Hill when she saw it, that had awakened the suppressed romantic in Bea, and she was convinced that it was sufficiently idiosyncratic to interest anyone with half a soul who was looking to change her life.

The old lady who'd lived there, had moved into the cottage when she got married in 1917, and stayed until she died at eighty-three. Three children had been born and raised and set free upon the world from two tiny downstairs rooms and two attic bedrooms. Her husband had caught TB and died there when he was thirty-eight and she was thirty-four. In the time between the wars the neighbours came to her for herbs and medical compounds mixed from her garden. She had delivered babies and laid out bodies. Rumour had it that she was gifted with the power to heal. As time passed by and the village died, and incomers moved in to smarten up the houses and commute from them to London, she became a local character, viewed fondly as the last of a dying breed. Patronised but neglected. Until she became a recluse. Ponies pushed fearlessly through the hedge to crop her lawn. Chickens kept the neighbours supplied with eggs. Her sheds provided shelter for owls and bats and the bric a brac of a lifetime in which she threw nothing away which might come in useful.

Mr Smith had lived there with her for years. No one knew where he came from. He was possibly a stray, left by the gypsies, who decided to stay. He was the old lady's constant companion as the years went on. Ugly by any standards, a skinny, coarse haired terrier, with a sharp nose and a ridiculous tail. His bark acute and insistent, enough to terrorise unwanted guests. His commitment to the old lady unswerving and devoted to the end. When she died Mr Smith went into mourning. His ears dropped. His tail lost its persistent quiver of enthusiasm. He lay by the door whining sadly and refusing to eat. A cart load of bandits could have taken up residence in the front garden, he had lost the will to challenge them.

Bea didn't even know whether Harriet liked dogs, and to be honest Mr Smith didn't have much to recommend him, except a lifetime of loyalty and dedication, and the right to end his days in the place he loved.

'Are you Beatrice?'

Despite all her anticipation she was taken by surprise. When Harriet arrived Bea was returning books to the shelves left carelessly on tables by itinerant browsers. She blushed.

'I thought you might be.' Harriet stretched out her hand, her sparkling blue eyes flashing a memory into Bea's mind of other eyes that were equally blue.

'I wish I could say that my sister has told me so much about you. But she hasn't. Except that I'll like you. And we have things in common.'

Harriet smiled, instantly establishing the link between them of shared sexuality, the truth and directness of which stunned Bea after so many years of secrecy and self denial.

'I'm glad you found it all right. We're a bit out of the way here.'

Despite her attempts to practise her composure Bea was blushing and stumbling around her words like a gauche adolescent. But if she noticed, Harriet didn't acknowledge Bea's shyness.

'Shall I look around until you're ready to come? I love friendly little libraries like this. They don't exist in London any more. In London it would be easier to get gold out of Fort Knox than a smile out of a librarian.'

'You should meet the boss. He'll soon make you feel at home.' Beatrice laughed. Her heart was thumping against her chest so fiercely she thought that Harriet must surely notice. She knew that she was staring at the young woman in a way that must be disconcerting.

'I'm sorry', she stumbled.'It's just you look so familiar. For a moment I thought we must have already met.'

Harriet laughed, revealing sharp white teeth and eyes bluer than robin's eggs.

'Short hair, trainers and jeans. It wouldn't be surprising. I suppose we London dykes all look the same.'

'It's not that', Beatrice said, blushing again. 'And anyway, I'm not that well informed. In my day, it was waistcoats and men's trousers if you were one way. And cotton dresses, high heels and lipstick if you were the other way. I meant something about your face. You remind me of someone I used to know.'

Harriet noticed the blush that had gathered at Beatrice's throat, the slight awkwardness as she struggled to explain – without being too specific.

'Her eyes look sad', Harriet thought, 'though what a beauty!'

Bea had the kind of difficult face that suggested she had suffered. Or wasn't happy. The lines that cut her brow and saddened her mouth were etched in pain, though not displeasure. Her hair was thick and coarse, the blackness streaked with strong slashes of iron and strands of silver. She wore it short with no pretence at style. Her eyes were serious and sad, but with a softness, a vulnerability, that suggested they might easily cry. Her body was tall and strong and wonderfully erect. But uneasy and repressed, lacking all of Maggie's flamboyant confidence. Harriet felt herself to be frail and anaemic by comparison, imagining that if she ever buried herself in Beatrice, she would be sure to drown. She was saying something about the cottage.

'I hope you like it. You might think it's too primitive. I don't know what you expect' Bea said.

'Everything you told me about it in your letter makes me want to be there. I can't tell you how ill I feel in London. How much I need some tranquillity and simplicity and space. I wouldn't care if I don't wash for days. If I live on vegetables from the garden. If I read by candlelight and sleep with the windows open to the stars and silence of the night. London is so frightening now. I long to feel safe again.'

She could have been Lotta as she spoke. So like her to look at. So animated in her excess of optimism.

'I'll get my things' Bea said. 'Then we can go.'

She looked so beautiful as she stood by the cottage door. Even Mr Smith rallied to her presence. He had grown even more scraggy since the old lady's death and was now surviving on the indifferent dog food he cadged from next door. He consented to a random quiver of the tail as she patted his neck and coaxed him out of mourning with the promise of a new companion in his life. She agreed the rent with the owner. Promised to take care of Mr Smith and the garden. Hugged Beatrice in her gratitude and pleasure and planned to move her things down from London within the week.

Beatrice took her to the station, long before it came to be associated in her mind with anguish. She watched her leave from the empty platform, the evening breeze ruffling her hair as she smiled from the retreating window. The train gathering momentum as it rushed towards London. Just as she had waved her final farewell to Lotta more than twenty years before. And watched her being rushed into oblivion.

For three nights Beatrice couldn't sleep, her thoughts were filled with Harriet and Lotta, fusing the one into the other like ghosts walking through her dreams.

By day she did her job with little interest and no commitment. She half expected Harriet to call. Though she had no reason to believe that she would. The telephone became an instrument of torture. Each ring a whiplash of anticipation, a stab of disappointment. She imagined Harriet packing up her books and piling clothes and favourite possessions into boxes. She wondered about her taste in music. Would they play Beethoven together? Or Billie Holiday? Would they play anything? Lotta had liked the Beatles when the Beatles were young and considered to be dangerous. When the BBC banned 'Please Please Me' and Sister Thomas confiscated their tickets to a concert on the grounds that Beatles, boys and booze might undermine their sense of vocation, they'd spent the night in Bea's room instead, jiving to 'She Loves You' and discovering a new sense of vocation called lesbian sex.

The day Harriet moved in, Beatrice arrived with strawberries and ice cream and a bottle of champagne. She had planned her visit and her presents with careful precision.

Since meeting Harriet she hadn't been able to shake the image of her from her thoughts. It was a strong feeling, an unaccustomed feeling for Beatrice, whose inner life had assumed a complex discourse with her reading. In lieu of people, with whom she could begin to share ideas, she had befriended books and taken to writing in her diary and to her pen friends.

She wasn't much interested in the thoughts of men, though it came as quite a revelation to her that feminists had developed sound theories to explain the historic domination and control of ideas by generations of male scholars and writers. Once persuaded, she resolved to restore the balance in her own reading, and give no more energy or thought to their perceptions, until she'd read at least a thousand books by women. She even came to feel their presence on her shelves to be offensive, as though her space was being stolen and her thoughts invaded.

One evening she had piled the lot into cardboard boxes and donated them to Oxfam. She knew this partial exorcism left their influence in tact to be implanted in the minds of others. But her loyalty to freedom and her love of books prevented action that was any more destructive. Once gone, she resolved to fill the vacancy with women. With the avarice of an addict she watched the dark green covers of her cache of Virago Classics multiply along the shelves, as she retreated into the lives of women whose words had long since disappeared and were now clamouring to be recovered.

When she wrote to Helen she talked about her discoveries. That Charlotte Perkins Gilman knew about the abuse of domestic labour and the repression of women's intellect long before Virginia Woolf was driven mad, and before feminism was rediscovered in the colleges and kitchens of America and Europe fifty years later.

'Wait till you meet Harriet', Helen had written back. 'She's the only woman I know who would happily retreat into antiquity if it meant she could sleep with Vita Sackville West or swap stories of obsession with Emily Bronte.'

Beatrice planned on strawberries and champagne because she didn't want Harriet to think she was boring, and because she suspected the only way to survive the simplicity of Heather Hill was to indulge in frequent bouts of self indulgence. She picked twigs from the hedgerow for the table. Harriet had beamed with delight. Bea smiled fondly. She was not a total innocent after all. Not when her heart was set upon romance.

Beatrice and Harriet

'Do you think Maisie's craziness is catching?' Bea asked Harriet, as they watched her run off into the snow, focused on some secret exploration of her own. It was about a year since Harriet had first written to Beatrice and come to live at Heather Hill.

In the night had come snow. Creeping like a thief. Intent upon deception. Large whispy flakes, creased with splinters of silver light, fell silently to earth. One upon the other in their millions, until the rough dry tufts of heather sank from sight. Until gorse and broom struggled to hold steady against the strain. Black twigs cracking, sharp and crystallised with ice, wearing their unaccustomed habits like an awkward novice at a midnight mass. The snow fell soundlessly and still, watched only by irresolute ponies, sheltering in sand dunes beside trees. Clustering together to collect warmth and consolation from the rub of winter's war on all who live outside of ordered domesticity and recognised boundaries.

The snow brought with her sounds of silence to the Forest, muffling earth and trees alike with a thick eiderdown of quiet. Brightening the daybreak with a dense reflected sheen.

Harriet woke earlier than usual, cheated by the unexpected brightness at the window. The roofs across the heathland lost in a mass of virgin snow and low white cloud. Her garden buried in an avalanche of feathers, with only the dry, dead spikes of lavender and lupin poking through, like skeletons in a wasteland. No birds were singing. The more adventurous of ponies, who bravely pushed inside the gate beside the broken fence, were, this morning, nowhere to be seen. Their backs turned in against the snow, their bodies challenged by the winter's first serious assault.

This was Harriet's first winter in the Forest. Each shift in the season bringing it's own treasury of smells and shades of light. She noted each with care, watching the early umber of the moor change to red and green and ochre, before seeping into brown and black again. Now all lay buried in a shroud of white. But sparkling and gay as the pale yellow sunlight struggled to position glints of diamond and opal in what would otherwise look grey.

Maggie was still asleep. Her head turned to the wall. Her breathing regular and deep. Harriet watched her sleeping, wondered who she was, what she was doing in her bed. She valued the two or three hours she could count on for herself before Maggie, the self proclaimed incumbent of executive stress, surfaced with requirements for coffee strong and black and buttered toast and jam.

She pulled on an extra sweater and thick warm leggings under knee length boots. Pushing the door to shift the drift of snow that had blown against the outside edge. Like a child she made her first careful steps, feeling the scrunch of crisp dry snow beneath her boot. Marking the line she travelled to the gate. Imagining the track she'd cut across the moor. The trouble she'd take to twist and turn and retrace her steps to disguise their destination. She sounded like a woman on the run. In spirit if not in substance.

And yet she didn't want to run away from here. She loved the cottage. Old by any standards. Its walls packed solidly together from clay and straw centuries beforehand. Its roof a heavy mellow crown of local thatch. The whole derived from earth and under earth. Related to the soil. The kith and kin of changing seasons. The friend of nature, whose shelter and solid endurance she felt would always keep her safe. Often as she sat beside the table where she worked, or climbed the narrow wooden stair to bed, she stroked the rough hewn wall against her hand, feeling the strength of plastered mud against her skin. As rough and ready as a hungry lover. She couldn't imagine a living space more suited to her romantic obsessions, her fixation with the past.

It was more to do with Maggie. The urge to run. The need to spring the comfortable trap that had caught her unprepared, held her with promises of repentence, and that now seemed overlaid with mixed feelings of dependency and compassion. Caught up in some confusing dance. At once intimate and compelling but flawed with a rythm that sounded a discordant beat. She was drawn to Maggie's arrogance and her capacity to make things happen. She was flattered by her jealousy and refusal to let go. She knew that, although Maggie treated her badly, she couldn't actually function very well without her. Power has its contradictions and weakness, its unexpected strengths. But Harriet also felt unsafe. She feared for her survival. Each time she waivered seemed like an erasure from which she would ultimately fade without trace. Still wedded to the dance, she felt like an accomplice in her own abduction.

Outside icicles hung from the thatch, glistening like crystal chandeliers in the pale yellow sunlight. She rolled a little ball into a fat body of snow. Making a smaller one to balance on the top. A precarious head on sound limbs. A snow woman she could relate to.

Harriet rang Beatrice.

'Have you seen the weather? What's it like with you?'

Bea was making coffee and contemplating croissants. Maisie was counting knives and forks on to the table as though a regiment was arriving.

'I'm looking forward to some peace and quiet and Maisie's expecting a bus load for breakfast'.

'Do you want to come over for a walk? Maggie hates the snow. She may not come. But it looks so mysterious across the moor, I'd like to show you'.

'I'll have to bring Maisie.'

'That's fine. Meet me by the pond at noon.'

Maisie, for all her skinny frailty, was no invalid. She bustled along beside Harriet and Bea, chattering at random. Harriet had put her in charge of Mr Smith. They made an odd couple as they darted off into the snow.

'Don't worry', Bea said, 'It's not logical. You don't need to answer over much. Just so she feels included. Do you think its catching, her craziness?'

'There are so many kinds of madness', Harriet said. 'Both of us are also crazy in our way.'

'Yes but my thoughts and actions are logical. I know what's happening to me.'

As she said it, Bea knew it to be untrue. The ways in which her mind filled with images and urgency was not within her control. The way her stomach tightened and tension gathered in her shoulders were responses not of her choosing. Her feelings were like delicate antennae; her senses out on stalks; her attention to nuance, gesture, absence was immediate and poignant. Her mood shifts as dramatic as a hurricane at sea. Her propensity to cry surprising and unrestrained.

'I look at the world', said Harriet, 'and it seems a strange and curious place to me, as if I'm no longer part of it.' She slipped her arm through Bea's. Her body softened against Bea's shoulder, as they scrunched the snow beneath their feet. Bea's heart beat faster as she felt the warmth of Harriet's touch.

These moments of gentleness and intimacy seemed rare between them now. Harriet was fiercely independent, slippery as a silver fish when it came to revelations about herself. As if information given would be control lost, would be power taken. Just at the moment when she most needed to be loved and nurtured, she was most likely to disappear until she had regained herself. Bea had become accustomed to her thoughtful and fumbled attempts to offer shelter and comfort being refused and misinterpreted. She knew Harriet had become wary of her love, had smelt the danger of possession and retreated. But Bea had no views about how to cultivate detachment, even in pursuit of self protection. Although her feelings of rejection were enormous, she seemed unable to stop, unable to resist the tender gesture of affection, the desire to stroke and comfort, to surround with presents that might please, to saturate with gentleness. But most of which now lingered, frozen at the point of action. Because Harriet was so prickly and Bea was so shy.

Instead the desires swelled like fantasies in her mind. In which she imagined holding Harriet's often worried face between her hands and kissing the sadness from her eyes. She imagined them preparing food together and sitting in candlelight to eat and talk about their lives and dreams. She imagined Harriet turned in sleep upon her pillow, in Bea's old brass bed in the attic, where the sun came early through the tiny leaded windows and birds tapped at the glass for food. She imagined waking first and bringing juice and figs and croissants back to bed. To see Harriet's lazy, drowsy smile as she surfaced against the starched crisp sheets, her arms reaching out to Bea. All the sadness gone.

Sometimes when she was lonely and hurt by Harriet's persistence in being 'already busy', 'just leaving', 'needing space', she imagined a battle raging between them in which fractured communications were like troop movements. Shifting to safer ground, into the trenches, on to red alert, measuring the advantage, risking defeat. Anger and hostility simmered as she imagined Harriet engaged in a self conscious game with Bea's affections. A scenario which could only imply that Harriet intended to confuse and took perverse pleasure in inflicting pain.

But in other moods she knew Harriet was oblivious to the enormity of her obsession. How could she know the countless schemes and fantasies woven inside a lonely mind? Or be held reponsible for not fulfilling what she did not know existed? Increasingly Bea's behaviour towards Harriet had become morose and grumpy. How could Harriet be expected to recognise that love and passion and longing swelled inside when, in brief, turbulent encounters, she appeared petulent and angry? She resolved a thousand times a day to be more detached inside, and to fill her mind with other things. In practice to be less edgy. As though friendship were her prime concern and passion was not a consideration.

But now, as on the rare occasions when Harriet softened, and slipped her arm around Bea with gentleness and in need, she was caught again, thrown back into the maelstrom, like a fish on a fly, drawn back into the complex web of speculation, anticipation and lust that was her intricate obsession. She resisted saying smothering things in case the fine thread of sudden tenderness between them snapped. But she held on tightly to Harriet's hand, sure to be the last to let go . . .

'How have you been?' Harriet stopped and looked into her eyes, searching for information. Bea couldn't even begin to say without blowing this precious moment apart in seconds. So she shrugged and simply smiled.

'What will you do about Christmas?' Harriet said.

'I don't know. The usual I suppose. Except I'd like to take Maisie to the sea in winter – before its too late. What about you?'

'I don't know'.

Bea sensed a shutter coming down imperceptibly. She knew her question wasn't entirely altruistic and that Harriet had drawn another of her famous boundaries.

Maisie was picking holly and grumbling to herself as the prickles caught her fingers. She'd tied Mr Smith to the belt on her raincoat. He was watching her with obvious adoration, listening to her distracted monologue as though, at any minute, he might join in. Maisie smiled as the two women came close.

'What is it again Bea?' She pointed to the berries. 'I can't remember.'

'It's holly, Maisie.' Bea said. 'Are you going to bring some home?'

'I am. I like this', she said, waving her arms in the general direction of the moor and the snow. 'No noises.'

'Do you want to go further, Maisie? Do you want to see the deer?' Harriet helped her tug another twig of holly from the branch. Masie looked towards Bea, unsure what she should say.

'Do you feel like walking some more, Maisie or are you tired now?' Bea never knew whether Maisie was up to making such decisions but she still liked to give her the benefit of the doubt.

'Let's go, Smithy. I like it.' Maisie and the dog were off again, stumbling across the moor.

Bea smiled at Harriet sadly, 'At least she hasn't lost her energy.'

Harriet took her arm again, reluctant to let the moment go.

'Shall I tell you about my search for Lotta', she said. 'Are you still interested?'

What a question! Her dear, precious Lotta. The love of her life. The most secret of all her secrets. It wasn't a question of interest. It was a question of being able to cope with the consequences of Harriet finding her. Or not finding her.

'Yes, I'm still interested', she said simply.

. . . For Harriet the search for Lotta was like a crusade. One night in her cups, Bea had told the tale of her first, and long lost, love. That had left her as lonely as she now was. And that had kept Harriet sitting on the edge of her seat with rapt attention.

'We were very young', Beatrice had begun. 'About nineteen or twenty, I suppose. We were training to be nurses. I noticed Lotta the first day I arrived at the hospital. She was leggy like a skittish colt. But shy like young girls sometimes are who've grown up in the country. She had fair, curly hair the colour of ripe corn, all streaked with grey and gold. her eyes were the clearest blue I'd ever seen. So sparkling I sometimes worried that she might cry. But she never cried. Only once. Her skin was freckled like a peach and her fingers fine and slender like someone who should be writing books or painting pictures. Not sluicing bedpans.

'As I got to know her better. I could see that she was a dreamer. Always full of wild schemes about trekking to the Russian Steppes or crossing the Sahara on a camel. She wanted to travel and would spend hours, her head buried in maps, planning routes to obscure places with romantic sounding names. We used to borrow guide books from the library and look up the number of mosques in Istanbul, the lunchtime temperature in the Valley of the Kings, the cost of a gondola ride in Venice. Of course we never went any where. We didn't have the money. Or the opportunity. The odd excursion to Whitby. A bus ride to Malham I remember well. But the training was hard in those days. We weren't expected to take time off.

'We worked on the same ward. Which meant we saw a lot of each other during the day, and what little leisure time there was, we spent together. She had grown up in a village, in a family of brothers. Her father drank too much and her mother died when she was fourteen. It was a miracle she was allowed to leave home I always thought. But a woman came to look after the boys, who then got married to her father. Lotta escaped when they started arguing about wallpaper.

'I was living in Newcastle with Maisie and her friend Agnes and my older sister. My father left when I was three. I never saw him again after that. Maisie brought us up at a time when being divorced was a scandal and earning your living as a single parent was hard work. She cleaned for rich people in the morning and worked as a waitress in the evenings. Sunday was her only day off. She couldn't afford to be sick and I never remember her being ill. She was so proud of me when I was accepted for training to become a nurse. She thought it was a step up in the world.

'Lotta and I were both glad to leave home. "Spread our wings", we said. We used to talk for hours about our dreams. The other girls were more interested in men. They developed crushes on the junior doctors and were always escaping curfew to go dancing and to parties. I think they thought Lotta and I were country hicks with no ambition. We thought they had no imagination, no vision.

'Then, of course, things started to happen between us. Everytime I saw Lotta I felt excited. I looked for her around every corner. Watched her whilst she worked. Sat next to her in lessons, saved all the gossip from my day to discuss with her in minute detail in the evening. She was the same. Her face, serious when she was concentrating, or engrossed in some task or other, would burst into smiles when she saw me, like the sunshine coming out. Like poppies blowing in the wind.

'I know the first time I kissed her, she wanted it too. We were shy, of course. Shocked at first. I didn't know that lesbians existed. She always assumed that you had to do it with men, but not just yet. Kissing her was fun. Her lips were as soft as petals. And she had a way of opening her mouth on me that made me want to melt inside. I expect you know about all of this'. Bea had smiled shyly. 'I suppose you think we were naive, even stupid'.

'I don't', Harriet had said. 'I don't at all. My sister says she always knew she was a lesbian. But I didn't. The first time I fell in love with a woman I couldn't believe what was happening to my body. Sex with men never made me feel so delirious.'

'That was it', Bea said. 'I was falling in love, and from then on, nothing else mattered. Lotta was the colours of my day. Everything else was monochrome. No one told us what to do. We just followed our instincts, I suppose. But I know that very soon we couldn't keep our hands off each other. Hospitals have lots of cupboards and corridors and waiting rooms and storage spaces. We knew them all. There was hardly a nook or crannie in that place that we didn't squeeze into on occasion.

'The rest were so pre-occupied with men, they didn't even notice us. Except for Sister Thomas who was in charge of the nurses' home. Looking back on it now, I think she knew because she was a lesbian herself. But she was a fierce, unhappy woman, who clearly had a problem about sex. Not like today. No sense of being, what's the slogan? "Glad to be Gay". Either she was jealous of our mutual fascination or she saw it as a cancer that needed to be cut out before it had chance to spread.

'By now we were taking bigger and bigger risks, increasingly oblivious to the danger, as our energy and

63

passion grew. Lotta had taken to creeping into my bed at night. Such ecstacy! We made love all night long, as quietly as we knew how, grabbed two minutes sleep, and were back on the wards next morning, fresh as daisies. Wearing the taste and smell of each other on our skin.'

Harriet laughed, remembering her brief, intense affair with Kate. It lasted only one short summer. But sleep was non existent and exuberance was fuelled on adrenalin.

'One night, just as we had begun to let our fingers trickle down each other's skin, the door burst open and the light snapped on. Sister Thomas, her face twisted and tense and angry, was glaring down at us. "Just as I thought", she said. "Just exactly as I thought. Get out of here Charlotte and go back to your own room at once. I'll talk to you both in the morning."

'Lotta looked panic stricken and I was stunned with horror, my cheeks burning; my heart pounding like it would split apart. Lotta jumped out of bed and disappeared as quickly as she'd come. The light snapped off and Sister Thomas left, slamming the door behind her.

'As I lay in the darkness my body was shaking, my eyes staring into the blackness. I felt rigid, raped, smashed, invaded. And terrified about what they would do to us. Then quite slowly and anxiously, the door creaked open again. And there was Lotta. Her blond hair caught for a second like a halo in the dull moonlight that crept through the door beside her.

"Sweetheart", she whispered.

"Darling girl", I answered.

'The next second she was back in my arms and we were clinging to each other like lichen to a rock, as if our poor lives were over. I can still feel her warm sweet breath on my neck, the dryness in my throat, the thumping as our hearts pressed together, impossible to prise apart by any one who should try to separate us.

'We lay like this for some little time, feeling better as soon as we were close again. Lotta started to giggle, and with the bravado of innocence, my body began to soften and relax as she stretched herself beside me. We started kissing, gently at first, for comfort, reassurance, consolation. But put us together and it was like fireworks.

'Too late. A step shook the corridor outside, and again the door crashed open. This time Sister Thomas caught us in the act. I thought she'd just about explode she was shaking so much.

"This I don't believe", she stormed. "Now you've gone too far. Are you mad the pair of you?"

'We were of course. Hopelessly mad. Crazy as kites.

"Out Charlotte", she commanded, "and don't either of you leave your rooms tomorrow until I send for you. I have no choice now but to report you to Matron. And that will be the end of it."

'And it was. Except that with nothing else to lose, we had nothing left to fear. As soon as the commotion had died down and silence had returned, Lotta crept back along the corridor and back into my bed. We lay until the dawn broke, gently in each other's arms. Without speaking or sleeping. Waiting until the morning came.'

'Three times', Harriet gasped. 'She came to you three times.'

'Yes', Beatrice smiled sadly. 'But that was the end of it. Next day we were summoned to Matron's office and both immediately expelled. Our parents were informed and we were given forty-eight hours to get our things together and leave. Lotta's father came to fetch her, his face like a gorilla, his mouth a hard angry sneer. As the train pulled away from the station it was the one and only time I ever saw her cry.

'I spoke to Maisie on the phone. She was crying of course. It was the only conversation we had about it. She said, "I'm not going to ask you about the girl. I've talked it through with Agnes and we think that's your business. But what about your training? This nursing was a step up." '

'What happened then?' Harriet asked. 'Did you see Lotta again?'

Tears gathered to the edge of Bea's sad grey eyes and ran down her cheeks like rivers of rain on a dusty window. It was some little time before she could speak, her body rocking as she cried. Tears she had bottled up for years. Loss and loneliness she had learned to live with. Feelings she had suppressed until both they, and she, had become invisible. A rich velvet curtain pulled across her memories.

'Never. I've never seen her since. Just a post card sent from York, of four young girls dressed as brides of Christ, at their wedding to the Lord. "What will become of us?" she wrote. "Thinking of you always. Lotta." '

'Did you know what happened to her?' Harriet asked, stroking Bea's fingers gently as she spoke.

'A friend told me she saw her in a tea shop once, working as a waitress. It was one of those old fashioned places where you have to wear long black dresses and white cotton aprons. She said she was looking well enough. But it was a long way from the Russian Steppes.'

Harriet had been completely taken over by Bea's story. Moved until she could almost feel the loss and yearning in her own precarious emotions. Bea's sadness touched her ambivalence. Somehow it sharpened her unhappiness when she thought of Maggie. All the deceit. The struggle to salvage a relationsnip from which her heart had already taken absence without leave.Finding Lotta became a kind of obsession, a crusade. A gift she might give to Beatrice. Possibly a touchstone. An act of faith in the possibility of romantic love. She didn't tell Maggie about her search. Or Helen. She didn't tell any one except Bea, needing her permission to continue.

'Shall I tell you about my progress?' she said. 'Are you still interested?'

Bea was looking wistful.

'Yes I'm still interested'.

'I got the address of a local history group in York from the library and wrote them a letter. I said I was trying to trace an old friend who worked in a tea shop in the late sixties. Could they help me? They sent a list of tea shops that were in business twenty-odd years ago, with the telephone numbers of those that are still going. Only two fitted the description of being 'old fashioned', which is a pretty thin connection. But I tried them first. Neither kept records of past workers. Why should they? Waitresses come and go with the seasons. But one of them, 'Nellie's', has a long tradition and the woman I spoke to was certainly curious. She said she was interested in family history. I think she was interested in women. She said an aunt of hers used to work in the kitchens in the sixties and might remember someone called Charlotte with blond hair and bright blue, sparkling eyes. On Wednesday this letter arrived. I've brought it to show you.'

Bea took the pale green envelope from Harriet and looked inside cautiously.

'Go on, Bea. Read it. It won't bite you.'

'It might', Bea said. 'Can I cope with this, Harriet? Do I want to be turned inside out again?'

'Read it, Bea. It's pretty vague. But it might be a lead we can follow.'

'You look just like her when you're excited', she wanted to say. Instead she took out the single piece of writing paper from the envelope.

'My niece tells me you are trying to contact Charlotte Simpson. I used to know Charlotte.

We worked together for about a year in 1968. She had a room above the cafe and worked as a waitress. I lost touch when she got pregnant and left to get married. The gentleman was a farmer. He came from a little village just outside York called Roe Appleby. I think she went to live there too when she got married. She was a nice girl. Please give her my best wishes if you find her. Tell her to get in touch.'

'She got married!' Bea was horrified. 'Pregnant! And she got married! It can't be Lotta.'

Harriet squeezed Bea's arm tighter.

'It's not surprising, Bea, if you think about it. A hostile family. Sacked in disgrace from the hospital. A bed-sitting room over a badly paid job. No contact with other lesbians. Everyone else her age getting married and having babies . . .'

'I didn't', Bea cried. 'I never thought of anyone else, man or woman. Only Lotta.'

'Well I did', Harriet said. 'I got married when I was nineteen, and I was from a generation that should have known better!'

'You were married?' Bea could hardly believe it.

'It didn't last more than a year', Harriet laughed. 'But

68

at the time I didn't think about it. You know about social pressure, Bea. Even though you've been strong enough to resist it.'

'You make me sound very determined', Bea said. 'I don't think it was like that. It's just I've never really liked men and I've never known any other lesbians besides Lotta '.

'You know Helen and Maggie and me. There are lesbians all around you if you only look for them. What about the woman with the dog that comes in the library on Tuesdays to change her art books? And Mrs Emsworth's neighbour? And what about Maisie and Agnes?'

Bea laughed.

'You're crazy', she said. 'And I've obviously led a very sheltered life.'

'Look there's the deer', Harriet interrupted, pointing to the clearing by the trees. A fine albino stag, well known in the Forest for his curious colour and magnificent antlers, gazed across the heathland to where the river split the Forest into water. A string of doe were scattered beside him, their rumps speckled with white, like splashes of snow.

'It still feels special to see the deer', Bea said. 'Even though there are lots of them here. They're very shy. It's a good omen, I always think.'

'Good. Some positive thinking', Harriet smiled. 'You're much more fun when you're not cross with me.'

She hugged Bea like an old school friend and kissed her fondly on both cheeks.

'Can I continue with my research?'

Bea felt destined to be ditched by the women she loved. But what could she say? Being friends with Harriet was better than being enemies. It was probably the most she could expect.

'OK. But if you discover that she's still happily married, and now has millions of children, don't look any further. And please spare me the ghastly details.'

When Harriet got home, Maggie was up and brooding. Pacing restlessly between the sitting room and the kitchen, nursing her irritation with a stiff gin. She looked like a caged bear. She was a big woman with thick red hair that swept away from her face in boisterous curls. Her strong features were dramatic and expansive, like the Forest in autumn, with wild green eyes, the colour of jade, that could splinter granite. Except for her colouring, which was all flame and tawny and alabaster, she looked Italian. Like a painting slashed upon canvas by Titian or Botticelli. Harriet knew these painted women well, their breasts heavy and enduring, their ripe marbled nakedness magnificent. To be buried in. To be consumed with fire. Her fantasy, when she considered Maggie. But unfulfilled.

There was nowhere in the cottage that Maggie could stand to her full height, and in three strides she had crossed and devoured each room. As soon as she'd seen Heather Hill, Harriet knew that it would not contain Maggie for long. Her body filled the tiny spaces that were created centuries before for smaller, less flamboyant people. When she was at ease, she looked like a character in *Alice Through the Looking Glass* who had outgrown her surroundings. When she was angry, as she was now, she looked like a caged bear.

'This place gives me the creeps', Maggie said accusingly, when Harriet returned.

'There's a feel of death about these rooms. You can smell it in the timbers. Finger it in the atmosphere.'

'Is something wrong?' Harriet said, 'Other than you don't like my house.'

'I can't understand why you want to be here Harry. A deep freeze would be warmer. Nowhere to wash. An earth closet. A very precarious association with the National Grid. You could go to Tuscany and drop out in comfort if you're sick of London.'

'OK. I'll go to Tuscany. Would you like that any better? You'd still have to wrench yourself from the water bed and the white sports car if you were to come and visit me.'

'I don't know what was wrong with London. You could have changed flats. You didn't need to live beyond the barricades.'

'Maggie I was sinking. Another term in that school, on that underground, in that flat, against that city, and I'd have cracked up. I like it here. It's timeless, fundamental, consequential. The wildness suits me. The simplicity eases my distress. The solitude gives me back to myself again, after so many years.'

'But you're not solitary, Harry. You spend most of your time in that damned cafe. In that bloody library. Trekking through the snow with that boring woman and her batty mother.'

'Ah!' said Harriet. 'So that's it. You could have come. Yesterday you complained when I woke you up to show you the frost on the mistletoe. You don't like snow. But you could have come.'

'I don't like that boring woman. What do you see in her?'

'Beatrice is my friend. It's immaterial whether you like her or not. If "liking" were a criterion, I don't even

71

know half the women you spend time with, let alone like them. I can't imagine why you should be jealous of Bea.'

'We made a promise to each other when you left town that we wouldn't sleep with anyone else, not without telling each other first.'

'I don't believe I'm hearing this.' Harriet was almost speechless.

'I haven't slept with anyone else at all since we got involved. I don't even sleep with you, if we're being clinical. And that's not my choosing. Whilst you ... You've probably lost count of how many times you've fucked around in the last three years. London is littered with the debris of well thumbed bodies you've discarded in your travels. Don't talk to me of promises.'

'None of those women has mattered to me like you do, Harry. You know that. I wouldn't need them if you'd agree to live with me properly, like most people who are in love choose to do.'

'OK. Let's talk about living together. Let me ask you some questions. Who cooks dinner? Who washes the sheets? Who cleans the split level oven. Who decides whether it's Hackney or Hampstead? Hampstead or Hampshire? Who is civilised and forbearing when the breathless message on the answer phone is from Sophie or Sadie or Susan or Sheila? Need I go on? I don't want to live with anyone. Certainly not you.'

'Fuck you, Harriet. If that's what you think. I don't need this aggravation.'

Within seconds they were into the now familiar flair of accusation and counter accusation, the hostility that had taken lodgings just beneath the surface of every exchange. Temporarily controlled, instantly alight, like the flash of a bush fire in a blistering summer. They were shouting now. Spiteful, angry, vicious words, hurled like shrapnel into tender flesh. Bodies taut like bayonets trained to hurt. Hearts pummelled by the ricochet of shrieking bullets.

The pulse in Harriet's neck began to throb, her temples thrashing with the pressure of her rising panic. Her peace destroyed. Her efforts to rebuild her fractured self esteem smashed afresh, like a robin's egg, fragile beneath a clumsy boot. She turned away.

But it was Maggie who began to cry. Her fierce, green eyes suddenly fearful and full of anguish. The roar gone out of her, like the rush of flood water through a broken river bank. Her body shaking with grief, her shoulders hunched against the doorframe. Her tears a random harvest after rain.

Harriet walked slowly to the kitchen and began to boil the kettle for tea. She took thin china cups from the shelves and piled a plate with cakes and cheese. Outside it was snowing still. The tracks she'd made earlier that morning already buried beneath a further layer of white. Outside, the Forest looked calm and rested under a heavy eiderdown of silence. The light was losing its significance, as the afternoon died into dusk.

She had wanted Maggie to go. Take the teatime train back to town. Leave her some space in which to recover. To breathe again. But she could see that Maggie was now in no mood to travel. The monsters were at her door again. She needed time to heal. She needed Harriet to pull her back from the edge, as usual.

Beatrice

Meanwhile back in Woodleigh, Beatrice helped Maisie and the holly out of the car, and across the snow, to the front door. She had entertained Bea with a ceaseless stream of consciousness on the journey back, about Mr Smith and the deer and icicles and Agnes and Newcastle during the war. Her pinched, crinkled skin was pink and bright from the chill wind, her eyes alight with happiness. She held on to Bea's arm and nuzzled her head affectionately into Bea's shoulder as she fumbled with the key.

'I like Harriet', she said. 'Your friend. She's nice.'

Beatrice also felt that a warm glow had settled somewhere around her heart after an afternoon spent with Harriet. She would have liked to go home with her to the cottage. Build a bright, anarchic fire and close the curtains against the darkness. By the light of the oil lamp and the exquisite poignancy of Delius, eat buttered mushrooms and garlic bread, and watch the logs flair and crumple in the firelight. Wear the taste and scent of wood smoke in her hair. Climb with Harriet the narrow wooden stairs into the eaves, where her bed, pristine under white linen sheets and beneath a carefully embroidered spread of peacock feathers and lily flowers, was the place she dreamed of lying, safe in Harriet's arms.

When she thought about Harriet's bed, as she so often did, and imagined herself in it, her fantasy was tender and modest in the circumstances. She always expected to be gentle. Never throbbing and aching and tearing and thrusting, although she knew such passion existed. Rather, she imagined tranquillity. Imagined Harriet unwrapping her from her woolly skirt and Shetland cardigan, her checkered cotton shirt and pale silk underslip. Releasing her breasts from the rigid organisation of her underwear. In her fantasy she didn't shudder with embarrassment about her lumpy body, or feel conscious of where her skin had broken into a million tiny creases and slackened against the sharpness of her bones. In her fantasy she felt beautiful and mellow and easy, her body like a warm, familiar temple in which Harriet could take comfort and find peace.

Harriet would lay her gently down between the soft white sheets, holding her eyes against any other consideration in the room, stripping away her own sweatshirt and jeans and T-shirt to reveal pale lemon skin, breasts generous and firm and unfettered. A cloud of yellow cunt hair and long skinny legs like a forest doe. She would be excited and laughing, she was at home in her body, as Lotta had been. Casually unselfconscious about her beauty.

She would climb in between the sheets, taking Beatrice into the hollow of her shoulder, and begin to stroke the lines of least resistance along her throat and inner thighs and hips, until she'd curl herself around a dream and be swallowed into sleep.

Maisie was sticking the holly in a teapot and searching the pantry for brown ale.

'Do you want to watch TV before supper Maisie, or shall we eat now?'

Bea was reluctant to relinquish her thoughts of Harriet in practical considerations like feeding Maisie. But she was responsible enough not to let the old lady become a hostage to her obsession.

'Beer and crisps', grinned Maisie, adjusting her woolly hat to allow a determined scratch, whilst searching the television channels to find 'Neighbours'. Bea decided to leave her to it for a while.

To say that Beatrice had never thought of anyone else or known other lesbians in her life was, of course, not strictly true. When she left the nurses home in disgrace, she went back to Newcastle. Maisie did her best not to complain about the qualifications squandered in pursuit of passion. And Agnes hugged her when she cried as though her heart would break. The word lesbian was never mentioned. The word gay, so far as she knew it, hadn't been invented. Bea struggled to make sense of her sexual feelings when all around her were images of normality. Factory girls in summer, flamboyant as a field of poppies in their bright, brash uniforms, giggling at the bus stop as boys shouted innuendo from the safety of the factory gates. The girl next door planning the detail of her wedding to a stevedore from Gateshead, her dress a pale shade of cream, which Maisie said spoke volumes. Prams and babies and shopping bags and family outings to the park, jumping out at her from every corner, like allegations of her oddness.

In truth she felt quite lonely. She had spent every minute of the day with Lotta and her training was busy and interesting and full of people. Now she was on her own. Her heart smashed. Her purpose gone. Too much time to think, she needed to find work. She wandered in an aimless kind of way towards interviews for shop workers and nannies and factory hands. Getting a job wasn't the problem, unskilled labour was greatly in demand. But just at a time when she had no sense of herself, she also had the conviction that she was fit for something better. Agnes encouraged her to study. So whilst she worked her way through a variety of menial and mindless jobs during the day, she spent her evenings at night school, learning about English Literature and History and Political Thought in quiet, studious anonymity.

She lost herself in books and began to rebuild her emotional life with ideas struggling in her head to make sense. She looked in vain for feelings that bore some relation to her own. For evidence of women who loved each other. For confirmation that she was not damaged or deranged. But all the talk in History was of men. Politics was a game played by men of greed and passion and charisma. Their big ideas about truth and freedom and justice were singularly masculine. In English she gravitated towards women writers, although the official curriculum was full of men, and the few women she came across seemed similarly preoccupied. Until Radclyffe Hall.

The man who taught English fell ill. And his place was taken by a strange looking young women who was studying at the university. Strange because she didn't wear frocks, or make up, or carry her belongings in a handbag. And she was curt and unimpressed by the two or three young men in the group who usually monopolised the discussion. She treated their thoughtless speculations about the meaning of Keats' poetry with thinly disguised impatience and used her withering predilection for irony to effectively silence them, so that the women in the group could speak.

For the first time since she began the course, Beatrice raised her eyes from the book in front of her and looked about the classroom to see who else was there. She listened with increasing fascination to the tentative and thoughtful contributions coaxed by the new teacher out of shy and previously silent young women. She heard herself laughing as the delicate wisdom and precise wit of Jane Austen suddenly became clear to her. She offered her own understanding of the plight of Mrs Ramsay and thought that if she read nothing but Virginia Woolf ever again, she would be content.

The young woman was called Miss Abrahams. She wore cavalry twill trousers, checked shirts, black, laced shoes and small, round spectacles. Her hair was cut short and spiky and she liked to stride around the classroom making the most of the available space. Beatrice thought she was wonderful, although there were constant speculations about her sexual orientation from the women and unqualified hostility about her arrogance from the men.

On what turned out to be her final class she asked Beatrice to stay behind for a moment at the end. Bea's face was suffused in blushes. Her heart racing like it used to do with Lotta. She could still feel the pull of Miss Abrahams eyes, holding her directly, in a way that made her blush and look away. And then back again to register the slightest twinkle of conquest. The moment of mutual recognition. Miss Abrahams laughed and brushed her hand momentarily against Bea's cheek.

'You've got brains. You should use them', she said. And raised a curious eyebrow.

Bea was too embarrassed to speak. Too shy to make the kind of response which she knew later would have kept this fascinating woman in her life for a little longer. She shuffled nervously, totally unable to make any sensible reply. Instead she shrugged.

'Oh I don't know about that' was all she could think to answer.

Miss Abrahams laughed again. 'I've brought you a book. It's not on the syllabus but I thought you might enjoy it. Do you know Radclyffe Hall?'

'No' Bea stumbled. 'No I've never heard of him'.

'Her' Miss Abrahams smiled. 'Marguerite Radclyffe Hall. Would I encourage you to read men? You can keep the book if you like. It might appeal to you.'

After that she was gone.

The real teacher was back on Monday and things returned pretty much to normal. The young men felt free to hold forth again with confident ignorance and Beatrice returned her eyes to the desk in front of her. Except that over the weekend she had travelled in her imagination into another world. The *Well of Loneliness* had engulfed her and she had discovered Stephen Gordon.

Having access to no further information, and only

furtive contact with the lesbian community, she identified instead with the tormented and ultimately misguided figure of Stephen. The perfect English 'gentleman'. Principled and self sacrificing. She imagined her with Eton crop, black suit and cigarette holder, looking much like Miss Abrahams. Bea measured her own appearance against the model of her heroine.

She was working in an office at the time which required her to wear skirts. To shave her legs and curl her hair. To dust a smattering of powder across strong cheek bones and a smudge of red across warm wet lips. But on Friday night she became transformed. The weekly disguise was hurled into the closet until Monday morning. Over the weekend she became herself. Or herself much influenced by her attraction to Miss Abrahams and Stephen Gordon.

Maisie and Agnes made no comment as she emerged from her room in waistcoat and brogues, her hair greased back with Brylcream, a delicate silk cravat knotted at the neck of her checkered shirt. She took to smoking Black Russian cigarettes and made the odd, tentative outing to one of Newcastle's oldest and most specific of haunts, the Queen's Head.

The pub was owned by a turbulent partnership and frequented mainly by men. Mostly they were oblivious to Beatrice. Some, dressed as women, flirted with her. But the subtleties of camp were lost on Bea. She wanted to meet women like herself. She wanted to come home. On Saturdays in an upstairs room the gay women of Newcastle gathered for the fray. It was a fraught, tempestuous affair with considerable anguish, jealousy, rivalry and secrecy the main ingredients of the evening. The first time Beatrice went to the pub she sat in a corner, shaking behind a copy of the *Exchange and Mart*, pretending to read. Terrified that someone would ask her to dance.

Relationships were begun and ended at the Queen's Head. Sex negotiated, rivalry re-enacted, roles rehearsed. The toilets smelled of Brylcreem and Max Factor. Someone was always crying in the shadows. Sex was always happening noisily in one or other of the cubicles. Strong liquor got the better of many. It was not the kind of place to find discussion or politics. It was not the sort of place to find Miss Abrahams. The feminists and academics were pursuing issues in other locations. Sex discrimination. Separatism. The trappings of political lesbianism.

At the Queen's Head real lesbians had no need of political justification. In the safety of numbers they knew who they were. Even if, like Beatrice, they chose secrecy and subterfuge as part of their shady existence. Here women, butch and femme, watched and waited, dressed in code, danced to favourite rhythms, found sex and freedom. Sought acceptance and lived dangerously. At the Queen's Head married women took off their wedding rings for the evening and kissed each other in dim corners. Bea tried in vain to do the same. But much as she might want to, she couldn't shake Lotta from her thoughts. Each time the door opened, she half expected to see her beautiful face. No amount of drink and seduction could persuade her into bed with anyone else. In the end it all felt too painful. Lotta was gone, and so far as she could see, there was no consolation to be found. Anywhere.

Outside in the black night sky, an owl hooted in singular splendour. Beatrice had now grown used to solitude and loneliness as a way of life. At forty-five it was less easy to be hopeful. Life seemed patterned by her past. Opportunities restrained by previous defeats.

'Maybe it's something to do with time', she speculated. 'And intimations of mortality.'

She felt a rising panic at the prospect of her life slipping away. To what end? Why had she been so cautious? For whom had she been waiting? Who knew that she existed? Who, except for Maisie, would miss her if she disappeared? She pulled the curtains against the snow black sky and lit the oil lamp on the desk.

'Its as though my life has meant nothing.'

A life wasted like a fine linen cloth wrapped in tissue paper and folded at the bottom of a captain's trunk. Unused and ultimately useless.

'Perhaps I should have been more ambitious', she considered. 'Developed some personal esteem through work. Made something of my life like that.'

Her studies led her into libraries and she completed her training with little difficulty. She worked in Newcastle for a while and then surprised everyone, herself included, by moving to Woodleigh in the New Forest. Just about as far away from home as she could go. She liked the life and took pleasure in discovering the serenity of the countryside after the noise and bustle of a big city.

But she was not ambitious. She did her job with conscientious dedication. Retreating when her tentative suggestions for improvements were impatiently dismissed by her superiors. Despite their discouragement, though, she kept abreast of new developments and attended courses at her own expense. If there was any justice to be had, she should have been appointed Chief

Librarian in her turn. The time that Mr Parkinson got the job, for example. But by then she had become invisible, predictable, a permanent amenity. Another unread book upon the shelves. The Appointments Committee was surprised to receive her application. They couldn't imagine her in a leadership position. Bea accepted the slight with resignation, though not with equanimity. It added another layer of rejection to the increasingly precarious balance of her personal esteem, and to the feelings of panic that gathered in her breast when she thought about the growing insignificance of her existence.

But by then there was Maisie to consider. Bea's sister Morag had seen the change in Maisie once Agnes died. At first she put it down to grieving. And to an understandable reluctance to cook and clean and shop with just herself to care about. But she was becoming forgetful in ways that put her life at risk. She'd forget to light the gas or leave pans to boil dry on the stove. Run out into the night half dressed, crying out for Agnes to come home.

'I've sorted out a nursing home', Morag wrote to Beatrice. 'I can't have her to stay with me. The boys wouldn't like it and Richard needs to relax when he gets home in the evening. It's the best solution. She wouldn't come to you. It's too far away from everything she knows.'

Bea was shocked to see her mother so diminished. Maisie who had been so strong and endlessly resilient. The colossus of Bea's early life. Her first and most enduring love. She went with Morag to the nursing home. Unprepared for what she'd find. It was a sunny Easter Sunday. The sky a pale blue wash. The sun a charge of iridescent yellow against the slight suggestion of a cloud. Someone had arranged tulips in the hallway, white fringed with mauve. Red smudged with yellow. Their languorous stems reaching in delicate confusion towards the sunlight. It was not an unpleasant place. But it grieved Bea to think her mother's life had come to this.

In the day room a cluster of old ladies sat grouped around the television. Each locked into her own confusion. Some blank, some restless eyes focused on the flickering screen. They were watching an Indian film with sub titles. Since none could read the words and none was Indian, the activity seemed less than fruitful. Maisie's head was hung in sleep. Her tiny body dressed in pink Crimpline was propped precariously against scarlet cushions on a green velvet chair.

Bea could feel the tears stinging at her eyes, the breath catching in her throat.

'She can't stay here Morag. No one should resort to this.'

Morag was unmoved.

'There's no alternative, Beatrice. You tell me what else we can do.'

Bea knelt beside her mother's chair and stroked her fingers gently until she stirred. The old lady smiled in recognition before huge tears gathered in the corners of her eyes and splashed down her cheeks along the creases of her wrinkles.

'Take me home, Bea. I want to live with you and Agnes, like we used to be. This place smells of dying flesh. I'm not ready for this yet.'

'But you'll be safe here, Maisie. They'll look after you. No need to struggle on your own, my poppet.'

'I'll run amok Bea. I'm telling you. You think I'm crazy? You've seen nothing yet. You get me out of here before I burn it down.'

Her eyes twinkled. She knew Bea was not like Morag

who was unmoved by passion, icy to the core like her godforsaken father.

'Will you mind moving south Maisie? My home is there now. I can't come back to Newcastle. But you can come and live with me if that's what you want.'

'Can Agnes come too? She's looked after you for long enough.'

'You know she's dead now Maisie. But you can bring all her pictures and her things to keep you company.'

'Dead? That's what you think. She's just keeping out the way. She'll come in her own time. You wait and see.'

Bea patted her hand. Aware that any coherence had now a tenuous relation to the truth.

'I'll go and speak to the Matron and see how soon you can be moved.'

That was five years ago now. Since which time Maisie had taken to her liberation like a child to sunshine. Except for the confusion in her mind, she was as fit as a frog and frisky as a rabbit. Not a day's sickness since she arrived. Not a suggestion of a cold. The only person Bea knew who had escaped last winter's flu.

'Its the air down here', Maisie said a few days later at breakfast. Bea was reading a card that had arrived from Harriet. Confusing her as usual with the obscurity of it's contents.

'What's that Maisie? What about the air?'

'It makes you crazy. Harriet's crazy. So are you.' Maisie laughed.

'I think you could be right, old girl.'

Bea pinned the postcard to the noticeboard and wiped the egg from Maisie's chin.

Beatrice

The pavement was splashed with yellow light. The sleet slid beneath uneven flags of bruised stone. Polished by decades of relentless feet. Leaning against the wind that blew in from the river. Pulling against the hill that climbed to the church and the Masonic Hall at the top of the town. It was half day closing at the library and Beatrice was wandering aimlessly about the streets. The day centre staff had brought Maisie and some of the other members Christmas shopping, and she'd agreed to meet up with them later at the Magnolia Cafe.

In the town Christmas had already begun to arrive.

Noisy children released from school for the holidays, were dancing and swirling across the pavement like crisp dry leaves caught in a whirlwind. Splattered by the sleet. Their parents shouting random instructions, cautions and rebukes, as they struggled with bags of puddings and crackers, biscuits and bottles, out of uniform supermarkets.

The second home fraternity had arrived from London in cashmere coats and subtle shades of affluence. Their creased, confident faces already tanned from winter holidays abroad and the lick of wind in the Solent as their yachts swung against the squalls of ill tempered tides. The locals huddled against the wind, wrapped arm in arm in a flurry of expectations. Cousins and nieces and sons heading home from the north. To be bundled into Christmas parties and pantomimes with the planned precision of a well repeated ritual.

Beatrice felt lonely. As she often did on the periphery of family life. And what seemed like her exclusion from the communal purpose of all about her. To walk along the street laughing. To be engrossed in mutual intimacy. To feel cherished by feelings as poignant, as massive as her own. Were all absences in her life. She felt unloved. A feeling she had grown used to. And had come almost to tolerate. Until Harriet arrived and sliced into her defences with the accuracy of a laser beam, the cutting edge of sharp steel. Her loneliness, so long suppressed, now riding on the brim of her tears. Buffeting her precarious emotions like a feather on the breeze. Until she felt out of control.

Originally the thought of Harriet had given her pleasure. Like a secret vice she could indulge in the privacy of her own thoughts. A warm place to retreat to from the otherness of the world around her. Her body felt alert and needy in ways she had forgotten. Thoughts of Harriet brought a rush of fire through her veins, her pulse quickened, her heart raced. Wetness gathered between her thighs like the juice from ripe plums.

But increasingly the need became unbearable. With every meeting, telephone call, exchange of books and letters, Bea became more and more intoxicated with the presence of Harriet in her thoughts and fantasies. She remembered the detail of every conversation. Registered every shift and significance in Harriet's mood. Grew familiar with her clothes; how she looked; what colours she chose to coincide with the image she was currently creating. She knew how simply and innocently she blushed. How easily her body bruised from careless bumps and grazes. Where the streaks of wheat and corn shone golden in her hair. She grew to know, as soon as she saw her, whether Harriet was feeling gregarious or private. Whether her questions would be answered, or whether each tentative advance would be treated by Harriet as a serious intrusion.

Bea knew she should let go. She told herself a thousand times that her response was an obsession. She'd lived quite effectively without love. She built a world with responsibilities and rewards that had their meaning. She didn't need pain and she wasn't deriving much pleasure from feeling emotionally ditched and damaged by Harriet's careless and inconsiderate commitment. But as with all obsessions, reason and logic are less powerful ingredients than the tenacity of longing and desire. She knew a dangerous streak of masochism determined her behaviour. But like all masochists, she refused to put herself outside the possibility of pain in pursuit of the possibility of pleasure.

Because the desire to be with Harriet was so always

unfulfilled, illicit longings had now turned into self pun-
ishing shafts of pain. Now when she took herself to bed,
with pictures of Harriet in her head, she cried as though
her heart would splinter from the inevitability of her
own loneliness. She could imagine herself drowning in
the pools of her tears. The boat she pushed out in
renewed hope floundering and sinking as it disintegrated
amidst the turbulence of conflicting currents.

She hadn't seen Harriet since they had walked
together with Maisie in the snow. Which was of course
the usual pattern of Harriet's unpredictable commitment. Beatrice knew no one so elusive. No one whose
reliability was in such direct opposition to Bea's concern
for contact. Like water through her fingers, Harriet had
no sooner come than she was gone. A million excuses on
her lips already sounding her retreat. Her departures
always creating more questions, arousing more confusion
in Bea than any information gathered from her evasive
presence. Bea thought she did it on purpose. Cultivating
obscurity like an enigma. Fearing clarity as though a
diva, stripped of her costume, might lose her mystery.
Might lose control.

On Monday a card had arrived which, like all
Harriet's attempts at communication, seemed studiously
constructed to reveal nothing. She who was so good with
words and at keeping things vague. Beatrice read the
message several times whilst Maisie dipped brown
crusty soldiers in her egg. 'Hope all is well. Or as well
as can be expected in the circumstances. I wish that for
both of us.' As usual Bea's name was spelt wrongly and
the address was inaccurate. She had to concede that such

carelessness was obvious evidence of lack of commitment. The picture was of a medieval manuscript that had some passing reference to women. Bea searched it for significance but could find none. She wondered why Harriet had bothered to write at all and what thought had prompted an action so devoid of substance. She resisted sending a six page reply, full of agony and angst, in immediate response. Careful of her own protection. Instead she pinned the card to the noticeboard in the kitchen and tried not to think about it whilst she resigned herself to waiting.

So it wasn't unusual as she straggled in lonely distraction along the crowded pavement, that her thoughts were otherwise engaged. They usually were these days. She stopped at the second hand shop where once she'd seen Harriet trying on a silk shirt and waistcoat. Now she couldn't pass by without hoping she'd be there again. But the shop was empty. Next door she'd once bought Harriet a tiny fluted vase, its neck fingered to a frill like the folds of a vagina.

'It reminds me of . . .' she had said shyly to Harriet as she passed it across the table in the Cafe.

'I know', Harriet smiled. 'It's beautiful. Thank you.'

Those were the days when Bea couldn't resist giving presents. She struggled to restrain her compulsion now in case her munificence became embarrassing. And since Harriet so rarely reciprocated, she came to view her urgency as obviously misplaced. Like all the other trinkets and endearments, she never saw the vase displayed. She had imagined Harriet filling it with pencils on her writing table or with snowdrops by her bedside. But probably it got recycled in its turn. As a present for someone else. Bea didn't care to speculate.

The faded hankie etched with daisies and forget-me-nots that Harriet gave her once when she'd made her cry, Bea carried around with her for weeks. Like a child's comforter. Stroking it for reassurance in the pocket of her cardigan. transferring it at night so that its musky smell, reminding her of Harriet's perfume, would linger on her pillow.

'What foolishness', she sighed and walked on past the flower shop where once she'd bought a single arum lily and pinned it to the windscreen of Harriet's car in the library car park. Harriet never spoke of finding it. Bea couldn't imagine how she wouldn't. Clearly she was so used to being courted, it cut no ice. Bea wished she could cultivate the same distance. Not that she had much experience of being the object of unrequited love. Only Mr Parkinson. And his ardour soon cooled. After the first rebuff.

As usual Bea looked for Harriet everywhere. Half expecting to see her, though she had no evidence that she'd be in town. She wondered why Harriet didn't search her out at the library or wait for her in the Cafe. She could easily track her down if she had the mind to. But of course Bea wasn't that important. Whatever fuelled Harriet's edgy, intense desires, that kept her permanently in transit and visibly unable to relax. That made her talk earnestly of solitude but dread the moment she was alone. Were needs Beatrice couldn't hope to understand. And Harriet was reluctant to discuss.

'I'm a great believer in talking things through', Bea had said when caution and resistance climbed between them like a dry stone wall. 'It's all we can do to understand. To breach barriers. Why are you so reluctant?'

'What's the point?' Harriet had said. 'Don't let's get heavy with each other. We gave no commitments. We have no responsibilities. Only for ourselves.'

Bea couldn't imagine a friendship in which caring and affection were so deliberately excluded. Almost as an act of mutilation. As if closeness might permeate control and destroy preserved defences. Attila the Hun would be more susceptible to gentle passion than Harriet when she was in this mood. Would be more likely to extend the hand of comfort.

'Don't press me Beatrice. Can't you see I'm sinking? It's not you. It's me. These are killing times. And we must protect ourselves.'

Bea had no real wish to protect herself from Harriet of course. She loved her and wanted more than anything to be allowed to show it. And to feel loved and trusted in return. But it was clearly not to be.

'Well if you ever change your mind, you know where I am.'

Harriet smiled weakly. Her eyes sad with unspoken fear. Her face pale and creased with tiredness. 'Dear thing', she said, and patted Bea's sleeve with mechanical distraction.

Across the hill, a battered yellow beetle, immediately familiar to Bea, was negotiating its way out of a tight squeeze. The local traffic warden watched with interest as Harriet threatened to bump the boot in front and the bumper behind. Her body twisted over the wheel as she tried to haul the reluctant steering system into a more finely tuned response to the intransigence of the available leeway. Her attention was focused on the task in hand and oblivious to the stab of jealous sadness that turned Bea's fragile grasp on emotional detachment inside out. Maggie was in the passenger seat. Beside the window that carried a publisher's sticker for her latest list. Bea couldn't explain why the presence of the sticker on Harriet's car made her feel jealous. But it did. It registered familiarity, shared interests, possession. A badge of ownership. She'd like to rip it off.

And Maggie was laughing. Her head thrown back against the seat. An exchange which Bea could only imagine. But which brought a smile to Harriet's face as she finally manoeuvred the beetle out from the kerb and into the road.

Bea watched as she swapped more animated banter with Maggie and tossed a wave to the curious warden before letting the car gather speed and slide out of sight.

Bea turned towards the Cafe. Her feelings a jumble of loneliness. Her obsession worn like a cloak of shame. She must take steps to rebuild her self esteem. Get back in charge of her life.

It was some time since Beatrice had seen Maisie in the company of her peers. And, of course, she was in her element. The Cafe was looking slightly dishevelled. The kitchen staff had gone home early and Ralph and Jack were beginning to clear away when the bus trip arrived. The doors were flung open, and before they had chance to decide whether or not they could be doing with any more cream teas or Christmas puddings before closing time, everyone piled in.

The centre workers fixed Jack with the kind of thera-peutic, caring-sharing smile that defied him to resist, sugaring their mass infiltration with a coating of creepy comments about 'the friendliest cafe in town'. He took a deep breath, poured himself a large glass of mulled wine and switched the urn to 'full steam ahead'.

Once their entry was secured, the centre workers grabbed large slices of carrot cake and mugs of coffee and made a bee line for the table in the corner at the back. Out came the cigarettes. Off came the beatific auras. And for half an hour at least they were off duty. This was their tea break.

Meanwhile the queue of dotty and demanding revellers jostled their way to the counter. All wanting to be served separately. All wanting to be served at once.

'Pot of tea for one, please.'

'Two mince pies, brandy butter and a pot of tea, love.'

'Pot of tea for one and two cups, Mister.'

'Is that a pot of tea for two then? In which case the price is twice as much.'

'No. We're sharing, Mister. We're hard up.'

Ralph dispensed with *Aida* and turned up the volume on 'Jingle Bells'.

When Beatrice arrived Maisie shouted a cry of greeting. She was ensconsed behind a large knickerbocker glory doused in sticky pink syrup and glace cherries. Her cronies were three old ladies with faded mauve perms and regulation cardigans in thick white acrylic. Maisie had been shopping. Her woolly hat was replaced with a green tennis visor pulled down over her eyes on an elastic strap. A pair of pale pink track suit bottoms stuck out of oversized trainers which, uncharacteristically, had been attached to the correct feet. She looked like a refugee from Reno in search of a one armed bandit.

'New outfit Maisie?' Bea smiled at her mother and nodded kindly at her friends.

'Jumble sale in the Masonic', Maisie declared. '75p the lot!'

Bea could see Jack and Ralph looking flustered against the barrage of demands from hungry and impatient pensioners. An old man dressed in a red plastic nose and a Father Christmas hat was shooting party poppers at some children on a table by the door. They sat in stunned silence as they observed the order and sanctity of the Cafe slip into turmoil before their eyes. Their mother hurried them into anoraks and mufflers and beat a hasty retreat. In the sink the washing up was piling high as Jack and Ralph struggled to keep on top of the orders.

'I'll have a cheese and pickle sandwich and an ice cream sundae, young man. Any chance you could be quick? I'm passing out at the back here.'

'Looks a bit short staffed, Maisie. Are you all right for a while? I'll just see if I can help.' Bea pushed her way towards the counter. Quickly followed by Maisie.

'Out of the way boys. This is a job for the experts', she beamed.

Maisie pulled on a blue striped apron and, with the odd flash of sanity that occasionally surfaced from the jumble of her mind, she said, 'Looks to me like the idiots have taken over the asylum. Sit down please', she shouted at the random queue pushing its way to the counter. 'Sit down please. This is a cafe not a betting office.'

It was not unusual for Maisie to busy herself with laying tables. She did it each day at the centre and she tried to do it all the time at home, as if in preparation for an army of invasion. Now, at last, there was a method to her madness. As the cups and plates were banged into place on cafe tables, the centre members began to take their seats, mechanically and in obedient response to a ritual they could all recognise.

'I've lost track of the orders completely', Ralph confided. 'Can you find out who wants what Maisie?'

'Tea and cakes. That'll do.' Maisie spoke with such conviction Ralph was persuaded to believe her. 'Got a tray?'

Jack took another swig of punch and Bea plunged her arms into the washing up. The centre workers squeezed into the corner, lost in conversation, as though on a different planet.

'Bloody social workers' spat Ralph across the dirty dishes.

Bea smiled shyly. 'I suppose they need a break sometimes', she said.

'Yes, but not now. I'm a commis chef not a care assistant.'

Maisie readjusted her visor to what seemed like a more raunchy angle and to release a sprig of wispy hair across her skinny brow. She had reverted to lateral thinking.

'Eat your cake, Charlie', she instructed the old man with the red nose. 'Been drinking again? It's time you stopped pestering those children. Just like my old man. Good riddance, I say. Good job I'm used to this life. Glad of the work, me and Agnes. Keeps us going.'

Miraculously, or so it seemed, all were now seated and intent upon eating. In good humoured reverie stories were recounted as they began to rummage through their day dreams for memories of Christmas shopping trips and cafe encounters in the past.

'Nice cakes', Charlie said. 'Like a second cup of tea Millie?'

Maisie scurried over to the table by the corner and

slapped a saucer down in the middle of where the centre workers were studiously engrossed in avoiding their responsibilities.

'Staff tips', she announced with the kind of authority that defied them to ignore her. 'Can't be living on love alone.' She waited expectantly.

One of the workers placed five pence in the saucer.

'Looks like you've got yourself a nice little job then, Maisie. We'll miss you at the centre.'

The workers laughed together at the joke, aware that their time was almost up. Maisie might have been dotty but she was not daft. She could sense herself being patronised at five hundred paces.

'Humph' she sniffed. 'It won't come to you on its own, old age. You wait and see. You'd better sort this lot out now.' She waved her arms vicariously at the random gathering. 'Someone needs to pay.'

Bea was piling the last of the clean plates into their place below the counter and thinking it was time to extricate Maisie from her momentary management of the Magnolia Cafe.

'Harriet was in earlier', Ralph said, 'with that woman from London. The one that looks like a mogul from Channel Four.'

'I thought they'd split up,' said Jack. 'Do you know what's happening with the other half Bea?' His question was innocent enough. Provoked only by an interest in gossip. But it caught Bea unprepared and breached her usual defences.

'I think that woman's hateful' she said. 'Harriet's mad to have anything to do with her.' She blushed, suddenly aware that her response revealed much more about herself than the object of Jack's enquiry.

'But I don't know.' She tried to retrieve her distance. 'Nobody tells me anything. Why should they?'

Jack smiled mischievously.

'She's quite a mixed up lady, that Harriet. Needs taking in hand, Beatrice. By a woman with experience and maturity.'

'And you're the expert, of course, in matters of the heart', Ralph was irritated by the sudden flicker of flirtation in Jack's behaviour. In turn revealing more about himself than any recognition of Bea's obvious discomfort.

'Looks like we've had our chips, Bea. Let's go home now. We'll be missing "Neighbours".' Maisie struggled out of her apron and readjusted her visor against the dying December light.

'Thanks for your help Maisie.' Ralph attempted a friendly hug. But the old lady stiffened in anxiety, as though invaded by a stranger. She moved to the other side of Bea. She'd had enough of company for one day.

'Well, Merry Christmas.' Bea looked embarrassed. 'We'd best be going now.'

The queue of revellers was gathering by the door, well fed and happy. Somewhere in the distance Harriet was chasing Mr Smith across the moor and Maggie was drowning in a double brandy. At the Magnolia cafe Ralph and Jack had returned to the magnificence of *Aida* whilst the social workers were trying miserably, and in vain, to renegotiate the bill.

Harriet

'Do you want to talk about it?'

It was clear that Maggie had no intention of going back to London for a while. The politeness that had replaced the fury of their argument the other evening felt almost as bad to Harriet. Maggie was half way through a bottle of brandy, a tight knot of jagged depression lodged angrily in her heart. Harriet couldn't bear to see her so unhappy and as usual was concerned to reassure and comfort her as best she could. She knew from past experience though, the damage Maggie's turbulent affairs inflicted on herself. When Maggie was sizzling with flamboyant humour, generosity and charm, she was considerate of Harriet's needs and good to be around. But it usually also meant she was being excited and flattered somewhere else.

Her bouts of depression and churlish petty jealousy coincided with the temporary lull in her romantic fortunes. In which work was pretty mundane and no one of any consequence was breathlessly attentive to her every word and whim.

'Why don't you want to live with me Harry?' Maggie asked for the hundredth time. 'You still love me don't you?'

It was a word Harriet found it difficult to say these days. Mostly she wished that Maggie would agree to let her be, remove her emotional baggage and complicated trauma from her life. Take a job in Australia and put the safety of a world of distance between them.

And no, she didn't love her as she once had done, joyfully and recklessly, in a way that had consumed her passions and her commitments without question. She had been bruised and battered too often by Maggie's thoughtless infidelity to sustain all the kind and loving feelings she had once felt so completely.

Though clearly there was something still remaining. Something akin to caring and fondness and compassion. A regret for what was gone. A tearing sadness about what was lost. An illogical, inexplicable longing that something could be salvaged. A crazy notion that if she understood enough, cared enough, Maggie might feel moved to change. Helen put it down to masochism and Harriet frequently thought she could be right.

'I never agreed to be monogamous', Maggie said. 'You know that.'

'Neither did I' said Harriet. 'And I don't want to be celibate either, but in practice it seems I am.'

Maggie looked away. Her affairs never lasted very long. Once the conquest had been achieved, they ended. She always came back. Flattered by the experience. Reaffirmed in her personal arrogance. Full of energy and enthusiasm for new schemes of work and daring commercial projects. Like an addict, high on cocaine.

She never wanted to discuss with Harriet who or what had happened, and would go to excessive lengths to camouflage her exploits. She became attentive and persistent with her gifts, and childlike with her dogged affection. But making love with Harriet was never a consideration in her liturgy of atonement.

'I won't collude in this any longer', Harriet said. 'If we're to have an open relationship, it's got to be based on honesty and not deceit. Do you think I don't know what's going on? Of course I do. I won't be put to one side and then taken up again, simply as it suits you. Simply to fit in with the storms and squally showers in your romantic upheavals.'

'It doesn't mean anything Harry'. Maggie looked distraught.

'It means a lot to me. It makes me feel stupid and boring. The fact that I always forgive you, and stop you feeling guilty, makes me feel weak and desperate and gullible. If my self esteem was any less, I'd believe there was something wrong with me. A sound reason why you seem desperate to fuck anything that moves rather than make love with me.'

Maggie sank in her chair, her face flushed from the brandy and the fire. Her eyes red from crying and drinking. She looked dissolute, Harriet thought, and ugly. Not so very different from a drunken, faithless husband.

'We know each other too well', Maggie said.

'Too well for sex? I'm sorry. I didn't realise that ignorance and innovation were the only circumstances in which fucking could be fun. I know you well enough to know you don't like to be touched, if you're honest, and that you never come.'

Harriet had now forgotten reassurance was her intention. Home truths seemed more the order of the day.

'It's not important to me', Maggie was looking defensive, almost pathetic. 'You know I'd always rather give pleasure to someone else.'

'Maggie you're talking about power. You give me no pleasure. You're totally incapable of sustaining the exchange of pleasure and passion above a cursory fast fuck. The reason you always end it, or disappear, is to preserve your mystique. You quit before the poor bugger discovers you've got nothing else to offer. For one who talks so much about sex and reads so much about sex and flirts so outrageously in pursuit of sex, you're actually a fucking disaster area when it comes to doing anything about it.'

'Why do you stay?' Tears of self pity and failure were streaming down Maggie's cheeks. Incapable now of deploying any other tactics designed to minimise her loss, to work to her advantage. In the end, when all her arrogance was swept aside, her power depleted, her defences breached, there was nothing left but weakness.

It was at this moment that Harriet always relented. The moment when she couldn't sustain the anger of her hostility, her feelings of betrayal, the pain of her continuing rejection, any longer. Like the partner of an alcoholic, a battered wife, a lapsed catholic, she couldn't quite give up. Although she knew she should. She knew she should sit severely in her chair on the other side of the room. Wait until the crying stopped. Remove the rest of the brandy. Freshen up the coffee pot. Make a clean and total break.

'I don't know why I stay,' she said. 'I don't think I can do it for much longer, Maggie. There's no joy in this for me. You need help. Real help. Help from someone who isn't emotionally involved. Not acolytes, or would-be lovers or even friends. I can't bear to see you so distressed. But I can't solve this one for you. I can't continue in a relationship with someone who, when they're fine, doesn't need me at all, and when they're not fine, devastates my life like this.'

But she got up from her chair and put her arms around the weeping woman, her selfless gesture of affection causing Maggie to shake and cry even more profusely. Her strong proud body crumpled like discarded trash thrown carelessly aside.

'Come on Sweetheart', Harriet said. 'Put the drink away now. Come and lie down beside me on the bed. I'll stroke you till you sleep.'

And she did. Her eyes staring in the blackness as Maggie slipped almost instantly unconscious. For a moment she knew how tender and how trapped Beatrice must also feel when she contemplated her life with Maisie. Except that she was not responsible for Maggie in the same way. She wouldn't become her surrogate mother. Her emotional punchbag. Her psychological support system. She had to break their strange interdependency before she too fell prey to the demons that damaged Maggie's capacity to cope.

Heather Hill was to have been her salvation. But it would take an enormous effort of will, and profound commitment to her own best interests, to do what still needed to be done. Sadly she felt ill-equipped to see the struggle through alone.

And then there was Christmas to contend with. She decided to deal with it by trying to persuade herself that nothing special was happening. She refused invitations to Helen's and her mother's and Maggie's and locked herself away with Mr Smith and her writing for the duration.

She unplugged the telephone, borrowed three volumes of the collected letters of Virginia Woolf from the library and filled the cottage with the sound of Mozart.

Only on Christmas Day did she venture very far away from the garden and the Forest. She dragged the dinghy that she found in one of the sheds on to the river, and with a pile of cucumber sandwiches and a bottle of champagne, she rowed among the scatter of tiny islands that spotted the neck of the estuary. A sulky mist hung suspended above the water all day, swirling against the shoreline and the horizon, meanly intent upon confusion. Swans and cormorants drifted in and out of the shallows. Serenely unconcerned about Harriet and the dinghy. She saw no one. Not a single boat passed on its way to anywhere. The rest of Britain, for all she knew, was otherwise preoccupied with the indolence, excess and domestic commotion that generally constitutes festive cheer.

The wine soon chased any residue of loneliness from her spirits. The peace was perfect. Her mood mystical. She could live like this forever, she decided. A recluse afloat amidst the mysteries of infinity. In just such moments of idleness and dreams, obscured truths sometimes surface. As at the point of waking from a night of fractured anxiety, in which options seem confused or non existent, suddenly from the mists of drowsiness and bewilderment, a submerged truth materialises with surprising clarity. She could see suddenly that she was managing Maggie. Not simply trying to sustain a dying relationship. Or loving her. Or needing her. Or wanting her. But taking responsibility for keeping her going. Adjusting her own interests and responses and desires to accommodate the fluctuations in Maggie's moods and temperament. Obscuring her own needs to satisfy Maggie's relentless search for reassurance and security. Tolerating the damage inflicted on herself as a necessary consequence of trying to support Maggie's precarious liaison with emotional stability.

Harriet's behaviour was doubtless generous and relatively unselfish. Increasingly unselfish as the measure of reciprocal pleasure diminished with the spread of tension between them. But it was also unrequited. And was preventing Harriet from making the proper break with the past, that she needed to do, to recreate her own existence in a more hopeful and happy way.

As she turned the dinghy back towards the shore, and heard before she saw him, the insistent yelp of Mr Smith, irritated by her lengthy absence, she knew she had to break with Maggie for good. Only by not seeing her at all could she hope to dissolve the emotional ties that kept her going back. That kept her continually and repeatedly distressed. That sabotaged her chance of freedom.

By the time she'd dragged the dinghy back to the cottage and satisfied Mr Smith's quest for sport by chasing him through the heather, darkness had descended. She piled the fire high with logs and fir cones and watched the flames dance among the shadows till the evening passed.

With the coming of the new year she set about her writing and her search for Lotta in earnest. By Wednesday she had some more news and decided to surprise Beatrice at the Magnolia Cafe. It was three weeks since she'd seen her, and as she walked towards the door, she was conscious of her heart beating faster with happy anticipation. She'd missed her. And things felt better with Bea again. Better since Bea was looking less like a dejected spaniel and Harriet felt less like the focus of her emotional aspirations. They were talking like good friends again, the way they used to, before the dreadful night last October, when Beatrice crashed desperately into the Forest in floods of tears, and Harriet vowed never to see or speak to her again.

It was after an earlier period of retreat in which Harriet had chosen to avoid Maggie and the library and Bea for two weeks and had been struggling with her self esteem in solitude. She had got a message to say Maggie was arriving on the train from London, and needed to be collected from the station. Harriet could tell that she'd been drinking heavily, and that whatever the status of her current infidelity, it had clearly ended in uproar.

Maggie was in a churlish mood, not pleased to see Harriet looking rested, light hearted and self contained.

'Have you seen the woman from the library?' was the first question Maggie asked. She could never bring herself to give Bea the benefit of a name. It would have been quite easy for Harriet to say 'No I haven't. Not for a week or so. Why are you so edgy? What's happened?' And make soothing, reassuring noises to coax Maggie into a more amiable, less hostile frame of mind. But she was angry to have her peace, and the careful reconstruction of her sanity immediately shattered by Maggie's mean and angry incursion into her emotional space. So instead, she too shot to the offensive.

'What the fuck's it got to do with you? Maybe you should get the next train back to town if you're coming here for a fight.'

Maggie crumpled. As usual.

'I'm sorry, Harry. Executive stress!' She tried a thin attempt at a smile. 'Too much Cote de British Rail on an empty stomach. I need to talk to you. No recriminations, I promise.'

'You have no need for recriminations, Maggie. I'm the one who's celibate, remember.'

'Harry don't give me a hard time. The shit has hit the fan at work. I'm in the dog house in a big way and I need to talk to you.'

'Get in the car then', Harriet said, softening again. 'Let's go home.'

Meanwhile Beatrice had also been drinking. She usually enjoyed a glass of Muscadet with her dinner, but these last few weeks she'd taken to carrying the bottle upstairs to her attic, and draining the last remaining drops as she attended to her diary, or poured through the collected works of Radclyffe Hall. This evening she was especially morose. No word from Harriet for two weeks. No yellow beetle at the station, which meant she was around. But no appearance in the library, even though her books were overdue, and no sign of her in the Cafe. Jack said she'd come in for a coffee earlier that morning, but had left almost at once. So she was in town, but choosing not to get in touch. There was no answer when Bea rang. Like her phone was off the hook.

Beatrice took the disappearance personally. How could she be like this when she must know how much Bea wanted to see her? When Bea needed to know that she was all right? After a second glass of wine she became convinced that she was hurting Bea on purpose. Playing with her memories. Confusing her with thoughts of Lotta. Flirting and then retreating, until Bea thought her rusty heart would snap.

That, or else she could be ill. She could be really ill in the middle of nowhere. And who would know? Maybe the phone was broken. Maybe something had happened to her. A third glass of wine and Bea decided to find out. She could hear Maisie snoring in her sleep and knew that she wouldn't wake again until the morning.

She drove her car too fast along the unlit Forest roads, swerving to avoid stray ponies that used the shadow of night to wander at will, their gentle shapes suddenly illuminated in occasional headlamps. When she reached the cottage, she could see the lights were on downstairs, and could hear the persistent yelp of Mr Smith beyond the door, disturbed by her footfall on the path.

She knocked, to no reply. She tapped the window. To no reply. She knew Harriet never locked the door. And imagined her inside. Choosing not to come and see her. She opened the door into the tiny living space where Harriet worked. Mr Smith was safe beyond the kitchen in the next room. Harriet's books had been neatly tidied away. A vase of dried leaves stood on the table beside the oil lamp. Her white blouse, with the ruffled collar, hung across the chair. A bottle of red wine was opened and warming by the fire. But no one was there. Bea had an overwhelming urge to go inside. To place the crisp white cotton of the blouse against her cheek. Smell the scent of Harriet in its folds and creases. She'd like to open Harriet's notebook at the last page where she'd been working, and read what she had written. Feel where her hand had touched the wine bottle, placed leaves into a vase, listen to the sweet, exquisite sound of Brahms that was coming from the radio in her bedroom, and was waiting, like Beatrice for Harriet's return.

But suddenly she felt like an intruder, like a sinister collector of natural specimens for an illicit hoard of butterflies or precious orchids. A spectre on the fringes of Harriet's privacy. An uninvited guest. A ghostly obsessive presence. She sobered into seriousness about the violation she was making. Suddenly ashamed of her behaviour. She felt grubby, like an old man in a dirty raincoat, prying upon schoolgirls. Or wanking in the shadows of a sick society.

She retreated quickly out of the door, back down the path, through the gate and off towards her car. Just at the moment when the beam of Harriet's headlights turned the corner into the road ahead of her. The Forest was quite black. There were no lights along the track and no stars. A thin veil of mist clutched the brown, dead stalks of bracken and gorse that pushed along the ditch. Only the headlamps of Harriet's car streaked into the blackness. Bea waited, feeling foolish and guilty. She didn't want to see Harriet like this. Felt too agitated to claim innocence. Or to pretend a fleeting visit. Too distressed to conceal her anguish. In the car Maggie was instantly suspicious and wildly jealous. Harriet was cursing Beatrice for her timing but feeling worried that something was wrong.

'Wait here' she said to Maggie as she got out and walked towards Bea's car. Bea watched her emerge from the shadows against the mist, like an extra in a scene from *Brief Encounter*. As she walked towards her, Bea could only see her young, anxious beauty, her body lost in a thick woollen shawl, which she pulled around her shoulders, against the chill October night.

'Are you all right?' Harriet said. 'What's the matter?'

Bea didn't usually arrive unannounced like this, or look so tortured.

'I wanted to see if you were ill', she said. 'I thought you might be ill. Or avoiding me.'

Again it would have been simple for Harriet to say, 'No Bea, I'm fine. I'm not ill. I haven't been avoiding you. I've been working and trying to get my head together. Sometimes I feel totally vulnerable and can only deal with it by going into hibernation for a while. That's all.'

Instead she felt doubly besieged. By Maggie crashing into her peace. And by Bea crying into her solitude. Both of them making demands on her she couldn't meet. Not when she felt so precarious and needy herself. And so she said, 'Don't hassle me Bea. This is not the moment for us to meet. I've got Maggie with me . . .'

'Then I'll go', Bea cried. Tears rushed down her face as she turned the car around and saw Harriet walk slowly back towards the beetle. And back to Maggie. Maggie who would now listen to the Brahms. Drink the wine warming by the fire. Smell the scent of Harriet on the pretty frilled blouse and bolt and bar the door against any further interruptions.

She pressed her foot on the accelerator and roared past them into the Forest, weeping as if her heart would burst. Lonely and rejected all over again. Racing through the country roads like a drunken yuppie on a joy ride.

There was no way now that Harriet could convince Maggie that she and Beatrice were not involved. How else explain such drama? So she didn't even try. Instead they argued all night and stormed off to their separate corners of the roof space to separate beds and to fractured sleepless anger.

She was still unclear about quite what had generated the volatility of Bea's behaviour that night. She was usually so calm and sensible. They didn't discuss it afterwards. Not once the dust had settled. Harriet pushed the thoughts of last October from her mind as she opened the door into the Cafe. Just as she expected, Bea was sitting with a book beside the window pretending to read. Jack and Ralph were laughing at some private joke and feeding each other slices of mango in a far from seemly or platonic manner.

'I can see your ears flapping from here', Harriet joked. 'What's the state of their love life today?'

Beatrice laughed, conscious that she'd been discovered in her most disgraceful vice. 'There's been a row', she said knowledgeably. 'But they're having fun making it up. I think they'll probably close early, if you take my drift.'

'A quickie behind the counter before home time', Harriet was impressed. 'How resourceful and inventive they seem.'

'Desperate, more like' said Beatrice. 'How are you? Have you been hibernating again?'

'Fraid so. But I've done lots of writing. And I've got some good news for you about Lotta.'

Lotta

The woman closed the door behind her and threw her rucksack into the back of the van. Her life was continually interrupted by traumatic departures. The urge to run. Chaos left resentful in her wake. It had been this way for as long as she could remember. At least until recently. But now again, she could feel the panic rising in her throat. The monsters gathering in the gloomy moments before dawn.

It took some years to settle after she left the children. She had no property, no money, no qualifications. She'd imagined getting work and somewhere to live where she could look after them. But she had underestimated the problems. Catering, shop work, cleaning. All jobs that paid in peanuts. Factories were laying off men and taking on part-time women at half the price. To get a council house you needed kids to be living with you. To get private accommodation you daren't even admit to owning a kitten. And the children's father wasn't eager to co-operate.

'I'll fight you in every court in the country' he said. 'You're sick. People like you disgust me.'

She found a bed-sit in a faceless neighbourhood somewhere in the Midlands. It could have been anywhere. 1930s pebble dash. Relentless, orderly streets. Two-tone Anglias pulled on to concrete slabs beside netted windows. Men who worked in offices. Women who collected Tupperware. Her room smelled of gin and cigarettes. She cried a lot and she was asked to leave.

She begged to see the children.

The man said, 'Possibly. Perhaps we could have tea in York.'

She saved her wages and checked the train times. Knitted socks for the boys in stripes of red and purple. Painted a curly red clown for the girl, dancing on an upturned bucket. She cried for her daughter, drowning her sorrows in whisky.

She planned her journey carefully, arriving an hour before the train was due. Checking and re-checking that she had the presents. Lighting one cigarette after another. Resisting the urge to drink in the station buffet.

The train was slick and loud, intent upon its daily flight to Scotland. In her day dreams she still travelled the world. In practice she took the bus to work and borrowed guide books from the library. The train was full of families heading north. Men lost in copies of the

Daily Mirror. Women distracting fractious children with food and colouring books and jigsaws. The woman pulled her coat around her shoulders, shivering despite the mild autumn sunshine and the artificial heat whirling from the fan above her head.

The journey seemed endless. She checked that her hair was tied back and that her lipstick wasn't smudged. It was years since she had worn make up. It felt thick on her face like a mask. Stifling her skin. She was unsure how she should look. He had called her a freak.'Do you think you're a man? You look like a freak.'

She got out at York. Retracing the steps she had taken many times before when she lived above the cafe. When she first met the farmer. When she had tried to concentrate on being 'normal'. The city still had its flurry of tourists, Americans and Germans mostly, looking for origins and reconciliation. She hurried down the hill and through the snicket to the park along the river. 3.30 they agreed, on the bench beside the swings. She could see in the distance the red and yellow of autumn jackets and woolly hats. Women full of laughter with their friends, their children temporarily distracted by redwood forts and roundabouts. The trees were turning brown. Her life like a leaf that the seasons tear off and condemn. Her eyes anxious. Her children nowhere to be seen.

'I changed my mind', the man said on the phone before her money ran out and the line went dead. 'It would unsettle them and they are used to having tea at home.'

When she left the clinic some months later the social worker said she was cured. But the woman doubted her conviction. Maybe she could stop the drinking. But she couldn't stop the bleeding. She could never dislodge the self hatred in her heart. The sense of life's tragedy and waste. For what? What principle had it been that made her leave? What conviction? What fear? What refusal to concede? She couldn't now remember.

That was more years ago than she cared to think about. Now she was calmer, wiser, even well travelled. Happy in her way. Until the nightmares came again. Her lover stood by the kerb, her hand on the bonnet of the van.

'Don't rush off like this,' she said. 'Talk to me so that I can understand.'

The woman faltered, fighting her inclination, her old response, the urge to flee.

'I won't leave you', she said 'But give me time. I'll drive around the bay to where the beach is sheltered. I need time to think.'

Her lover watched as the woman's van pulled into the road and round the edge of the cliffs to the sea. The garden needed some attention, she decided. And she went to find the rake to clear the leaves.

Beatrice

'I'm a great believer in village stores', Harriet announced. Bea looked sceptical. 'They've replaced the confessional as the fount of all knowledge and the source of all gossip.'

'So?' Bea allowed her curiosity to escape the tight rein she had applied since before Christmas.

'I wrote to the village Post Mistress and General Store keeper of Roe Appleby. A very winsome letter. Engaging her sympathies and arousing her interest. She's a fund of information about Lotta, or Charlotte Trent as she is now called.'

Bea twisted the serviette in front of her into a tight curl, fingering the end until it flowered into a ruffle. Harriet could tell she was nervous.

'First the good news. She's divorced. The marriage lasted only a few years. There was something of a local scandal, it appears, in which Lotta and the wife of the local butcher were seen to spend an inordinate amount of time in each other's company. The husbands got suspicious and heaved in the big guns. The friendship broke up but Lotta then disappeared. She's never been seen in the village since.

'I telephoned the Post Mistress and asked whether she'd mind giving me Farmer Trent's address. She didn't mind. But seemed sure that I'd get no information from him. She was right. He was most unpleasant as soon as I mentioned Lotta and spat some obscenity at me down the phone about filthy perverts. I think it's safe to assume that young Lotta, like yourself, was not merely "going through a phase"!'

Harriet's eyes twinkled. Bea looked away, a strange surge of excitement and relief breaking through the tension in her body.

'What about the child?' Bea asked.

'Apparently there are three. Two boys and a girl. They stayed with their father when Lotta left, but he wasn't about to let me speak to any of them.'

'So does anyone know where she is?'

'The Post Mistress rang me back the following day. I knew she was a good lead! She says she doesn't know where Lotta is, but that each year since she left, letters have arrived at Christmas and on the children's birthdays which, for the last three or four years have had a Dorset postmark. She noticed them because of the tiny spidery writing. She always had to put her specs on to see where they should be delivered.'

'Does she know where in Dorset? Goodness Harriet, that's the next county!' Bea was sitting on the edge of her seat.

'I know. Just think. Lotta could be less than a hundred miles from here at this very moment! The Post Mistress isn't sure where, but says the letters came as usual this Christmas. She also says the eldest boy has a birthday coming up at the end of the month'.

'Will she check the postmark for us?'

'I think she will. Aren't women wonderful Beatrice?'

'On the whole', Beatrice conceded, but she was not totally convinced.

'There's one more lead. Her eldest daughter is presently at university in Bath. She's studying English Literature, apparently. And guess what!'

'What?'

'Guess!' Harriet was beaming.

'Oh Harriet, I can't guess. Tell me what at once!'

'She's called Beatrice! Beatrice Trent! What do you make of that, old thing?'

Sharp, salty tears burst against Bea's eyes and ran down her cheeks without control. Harriet took her in her arms and hugged her.

'So shall we go on?' she said.

'What can we do now?' Bea asked through her sobs, her hands holding on tightly to Harriet's arm.

'We can try the young Beatrice. See if she knows where her mother's living. See if it ties in with the Dorset postmark.'

'Oh dear. Perhaps she won't want to be bothered', Bea said. 'Perhaps they don't get on. Perhaps Lotta wants to preserve her privacy.'

118

'Perhaps. Perhaps. Perhaps. All of these things are possible. But we won't know until we try. Let's risk it, Bea. Live hopefully, my angel.'

'Do you girls want a slice of mango and a glass of wine on the house?' Jack was looking obviously amused. 'I thought it was only the staff that made a public spectacle of themselves in this place' he laughed.

Harriet smiled.

'So you don't have the monopoly on queer melodrama! What did you expect? Yes, I'd certainly like some free wine. Would you Bea?'

Bea nodded, her blushes mingling with her tears.

'Oh dear. I think I've just brought you out in public.' Harriet's eyes glimmered with mischief as she watched Bea's confusion.

'Now there's no going back', she said.

'I know.' Bea smiled. 'Who ever said I wanted to?'

After two more glasses of wine, and a burst of Jesse Norman singing Carmen on the stereo, Harriet said, 'I think it's time you took some more of the responsibility for this research, Beatrice.'

Bea was feeling giddy. And therefore not nearly so horrified by the proposal as she might otherwise have been.

'Like what?'

'You're the letter writer. Why don't you contact the young Beatrice yourself? Tell her you're an old friend of her mother's. See what she says.'

'I don't know whether I can do that. I don't want to raise any ghosts for the child. It could be the last thing she wants to hear'.

'Be vague at first. Just because you've come out to the Magnolia Cafe, you don't need to inform the rest of the world that you're a lesbian, until you want to. Find out what kind of young woman she is. She might be a feminist. She might even be a dyke, for God's sake!'

'Go on, write to her!' Ralph shouted from behind the counter. He was obviously another one adept at the ancient art of eavesdropping.

'All right, I will', Bea said. 'I'll do it tonight.'

'Excellent', Harriet said.'That's excellent. Look, I'll give you a phone number where you can reach me in London if anything comes up in the meantime.Otherwise I'll be away for about a week. Shall we meet up again here next Wednesday?'

'Are you going to London then?' Bea couldn't stop the accusation slipping from her tongue. It was out before she could stop herself. She looked away. Certain that she'd blown it. Yet again.

Harriet was in too good a mood to be hostile, but a shadow crossed the yellow sunlight that had shone between them.

'I have things to sort out too, Bea. You know that.'

Her pride wouldn't allow her to add 'Like splitting up with Maggie. The final showdown.' Instead she patted Bea's hand and smiled.

'Come on, old girl, time to go.'

Bea arrived home with mixed emotions. Excitement at the news about Lotta and the thought of writing to her daughter. Corrosive jealousy at the prospect of Harriet speeding her way towards Maggie.

She imagined Maggie waiting at the station, looking

handsome and passionate. And Harriet rushing into her arms. Neither would have any reservation about kissing in public. Unlike Beatrice. So ultra cautious. Ultra boring. Faded as if she'd somehow vanished in the world. Unremarkable and invisible.

They'd go somewhere quiet for supper and eat by candlelight. Or Maggie may have tickets for the theatre. Bought as a surprise. And then back to Hampstead in the white Porsche. To Maggie's only bedroom. Beatrice couldn't bear to think of any more. She took a brown ale from the fridge for Maisie and poured herself a large glass of Muscadet.

Maisie was showing her a painting she'd done at the day centre. It was strange but surprisingly good. Full of strong, bright slashes of crimson and purple and orange, against a pale grey wash.

'It's me in the garden', Maisie said. 'Look there's my trainers and my hat.'

Bea would never have guessed. Except the painting looked hopeful and gay and Maisie was beaming with the pleasure of having done it.

'Stick it on the wall', she said. 'Like we used to.'

'Do you remember when we used to Maisie?'

Bea's heart caught in sadness as she remembered the way her mother plastered the walls with every inconsequential scribble produced by herself or her sister. How scribbles turned into awkward bodies and cheery faces and aeroplanes and circuses. Her mother reluctant to throw any of them away, however much they multiplied. Agnes used to take them down periodically and put them in a drawer. But a fresh batch soon replaced them. The girls and Maisie innocently conspiring to keep the makeshift gallery full.

Maisie's brow creased in concentration in an effort to

remember. But the random echo from the past faded as swiftly as it emerged, amidst the trails of confusion that was her memory. She reconsidered the painting she was holding out to Bea, already unsure about where it had come from.

'This is your painting Maisie', Bea said gently. 'You did it today at the centre. Look it's a garden, and there's you in the woolly hat. Shall we stick it on the wall beside the calendar?'

'Good idea.' Maisie looked relieved and chanced a swig at her beer.'Is it dinner time?'

'Soon be supper time, Maisie. Do you want to have a wash and put your dressing gown on whilst I get it ready?'

'No I don't', Maisie said firmly. But she wandered off towards her bedroom as though she might change her mind.

Once Maisie was in bed and safely asleep, Bea retired to her attic. She was beginning to associate herself with all the mad women she'd read about in Victorian literature, confined to their couches with 'hysteria'. With the anonymous heroine in Charlotte Perkins Gilman's story about the yellow wallpaper, who couldn't rest until she'd scratched the sinister, hideous stuff from the walls in an effort to release the woman, herself, trapped behind. Driven mad by her controlling husband and the mysogyny of Victorian values.

But Beatrice, mad woman in the attic though she frequently felt herself to be, was living with no oppressor but herself. She conceded the point in her diary, in a familiar mood of ruthless self examination. 'You've buttoned down your feelings and settled for subsistence. Eliminated risks and danger. Squandered spontaneity and passion in the search for security. In the fear of being abandoned ever again. You have oppressed yourself with the vigour of a Victorian patriarch. Not that abstinence has guaranteed your safety. Why else be so regretful about Lotta? So obsessive about Harriet? So jealous of Maggie?' She put the diary away. These were all queries she could formulate but none of them were questions she could answer.

She kept her letter to the young Beatrice brief and to the point.

'I'm sorry to disturb your studies and have no wish to intrude. But I'm an old friend of your mother's from long before you were born and I would dearly love to get in touch with her again. Do you know where she is and would you be prepared to give me her address? I'm a librarian in Winslow and quite respectable as you can imagine. Please believe me when I say that I don't wish either you or your mother any harm'.

She signed the letter B. Hawksworth in case the coincidence of a common name aroused the girl's suspicions or hostility. And then waited to see what happened.

When Harriet got to London she went straight to Helen's and spent the evening in convivial chatter about books and gardening and the benefits of living in the country.

'You should come and stay', Harriet said. 'Come and meet Beatrice and her dotty mother. See "all passion spent" at the Magnolia Cafe.'

'Do you want to be disturbed?' Helen said tactfully.

'By you. Of course I do. I wouldn't invite you if I didn't want you to come.'

'What about Maggie? How are things with Maggie?'

'It's a long story', Harriet sighed. 'As yet without an ending. I'll tell you later, maybe, when I've had chance to talk to her.'

Helen knew Harriet well enough to know when to keep quiet. Although she was curious about the current state of her love life, she knew she must wait for Harriet to tell her. No amount of careful questioning, however well intentioned, would prise information out of Harriet that she was reluctant to concede.

'Do you want some cocoa then, before you go to bed?' Helen said.

'No thanks. I'm so tired. I think I'll sleep like the proverbial top.'

Which she did. Totally oblivious to the agony of self analysis that kept Bea's night light flickering towards dawn. Or to Maggie, at home in Hampstead, who had just succeeded in seducing Polly, an editorial assistant in Children's Fiction, precariously non-gay and on the rebound from a miserable and broken marriage to a solicitor. Or that somewhere in deepest Dorset, as yet unaware of the intensity with which she was being hunted, lived Lotta. Blissfully ignorant of the events which were to shake her inside out, just when she imagined her life was settled.

Harriet

When Harriet arrived on the doorstep, Maggie was clearly surprised to see her. The last time she'd spoken on the phone was three days ago. Harriet was in the country and had said nothing about coming to town. Fortunately for all concerned Polly had just left. Not being as senior a member of staff as Maggie, she had to be in the office by nine. Maggie could recover at her leisure from her sleepless night of passion by claiming she was working at home. She didn't fool Harriet, however. Guilt was etched in neon lights across her face.

'Come in Sweetie, how good to see you. I'm sorry

everything's in such a mess. I haven't been feeling too well. A touch of Beijing flu, I think.'

She was clearly trying to engage Harriet's sympathies as a temporary diversion, whilst hurriedly clearing away the evidence of two breakfasts having been partly consumed not an hour earlier.

'I just seem to let all these pots pile up when I'm not well', she lied. 'Doesn't display me in a very good light, I'm afraid. A domestic slattern!'

Harriet was not amused. She could see without looking the shoes and sweater carelessly discarded by the bedroom door. The ash tray and the empty wine bottle beside the couch. The red light of the stereo gleaming from the cabinet, which Maggie in her amorous distraction, had forgotten to turn off.

'You shouldn't be smoking again if you've got the flu', Harriet said.

'I'm not.' Maggie answered too hastily. 'Oh that...' she followed Harriet's eyes towards the ash tray. 'Well just the occasional one you know. Executive stress.' Her usual excuse.

But Harriet hadn't come to catch Maggie out. And she took no pleasure in discovering her, yet again, knee deep in deceit.

'Can I have some coffee? I want to talk to you.' She walked through to the kitchen, ignoring the remains of last night's candlelit meal for two, congealing on the expensive rosewood table. She threw the saturated filter into the bin and piled fresh coffee into the pot, choosing Java Blue from the costly array of different blends arranged on the shelf.

'Is this strong?' she asked.

'It's my favourite' Maggie replied.

'Then it will be.'

There wasn't anything about Maggie that Harriet didn't know inside out. She watched her sorting through the dishes, as if removal of the evidence would somehow constitute eradication of the action.

'Why don't you leave it and come and sit down' Harriet said calmly. 'It's too late for all of that now.'

Maggie hoped she misinterpreted the significance of her choice of words. She smiled weakly.

'How are you Darling? I've missed you so much.'

Harriet looked irritated but she had resolved to stay calm, and to say precisely what she had come to say without being distracted.

'Maggie I've come to tell you it's over. I've thought about it all over Christmas and the New Year. And I've made my mind up. We can't go on like this any more. I for one don't want to.'

'Harriet, please!' Maggie rushed to her side. 'Harry don't do this to me. You don't know what you're saying. You can't mean it. Harry I love you. You must believe me.'

'Maggie, we have to end it now. Now, whilst there's still some residual affection left between us. Now, before we tear each other to shreds. You make me so unhappy. I can't, I really can't go on any longer.'

'Look Harry, I'll change. I'll move down to Hampshire too. It's just because we've grown apart whilst you've been away. I could live with you in the country and commute to work. Lots of people do.'

'Maggie I mean it. It's over. I don't want to see you and I don't want you to contact me. We must keep completely away from each other. Any other way is too painful. Do you understand what I'm saying to you?'

When she told Helen later that Maggie had wept and pleaded and promised to repent, she was not impressed.

127

'She'd devour you for breakfast, that woman', Helen said angrily. 'And spit you out again by suppertime. Now at least you can really sort yourself out and make a fresh start.'

But Harriet cried and cried. Huge sorrowful tears. Loud gasping sobs that shook her body from somewhere deep inside and somewhere long ago. She cried for the loss of love. The misery of rejection. The hatred of deceit. A love, once so beautiful and fresh, turned sordid and pathetic. She wept for Maggie. For the pitiful person she had become. Seduced by shallow glory. An artless dodger in the grubby world of flattery and conceit. She wept for herself. For the loyalty she had squandered and the time she had wasted. For the sacrifice of her own desires and the disappearance of her own identity. In the pursuit of a misnomer. She would be more careful in the future to whom she gave her heart. Think twice before she spoke. Be certain that never again, unless she was very, very sure, never to say those fatal words 'I love you'.

Helen let her cry. Put soothing music on the stereo and made a massive pot of sweet milky tea.

'Stay here just as long as you like', she said gently. 'I won't let anyone bother you. You've done the right thing and you've got no reason to reproach yourself. Things can only get better now. Just see how much brighter the world will look tomorrow.'

'You're looking weedy' Beatrice said when Harriet breezed into the library on Monday morning to change her books.'Whatever you get up to in London. It doesn't agree with you.' She was trying to be jocular.

'You're quite right Beatrice , as ever. But I probably

won't be going back there any more, not unless there's an emergency.'

She didn't look like a woman whose lover was just about to move in to Heather Hill either. Unless her grey pinched face and straggly hair was a sign of nights of abandoned passion with very little sleep.

'Are you all right Harriet. You look bloody awful.'

Mr Parkinson had stopped stamping books, irritated by the familiarity of the exchange between the two women. An exchange which could in no way be construed as professional on the part of Miss Hawksworth. He coughed to alert her to his irritation and to his conviction that she should be getting on with the work she was paid to do. Instead of gossiping.

'I'm fine Bea, honestly. Look I'll speak to you later. I thought I'd do a bit of work in the reference section. You can come and visit me if Count Dracula doesn't grab you by the throat first.'

Bea laughed. 'What did I tell you? I said London librarians have got nothing to teach him about bad customer relations. I'll see you in a minute.'

'Miss Hawksworth I've got a little job for you', Mr Parkinson interrupted.

'Coming Mr Parkinson.' Bea smiled again and pulled a face at Harriet. 'See you in a minute', she repeated.

The reference section had improved enormously under Bea's influence. It now had one of the best collections of women's diaries and letters in the entire region. Harriet was pursuing her search of nineteenth century romantic friendships between women for signs of explicit sexuality. She wanted to make her contribution to the "did they do it or not" debate.

'Queen Victoria and Florence Nightingale' Harriet beamed.'What do you reckon?'

'Well you know what they say about nurses', Bea laughed. 'Not to mention royalty. Harriet has something happened? Don't tell me, if you don't want to, but you look like you could do with talking to someone.'

'Maggie and I have split up. I don't really want to talk about it any more than that.'

Beatrice was amazed. She had grown so used to feeling jealous of Maggie. Had assumed such commitment between them. Had assumed that, whatever the difficulties were, they'd been resolved.

'That's your greatest weakness Beatrice Hawksworth', Harriet watched her carefully. 'You're so full of assumptions. Most of which are wrong.'

Bea stretched out a hand to touch Harriet's shoulder. Unsure what to say.

'Don't feel sorry for me please', Harriet said. 'I just want to get on with my life and put all of that behind me. The kindest thing you can do is to never refer to it again.'

Bea nodded as if Harriet's response made some sense to her. But of course it didn't. She couldn't imagine not wanting to be hugged and comforted if she was feeling broken and distressed. She knew the pain of lonely sadness all too well. When there was no one else there to offer consolation. In the end each must be responsible for her own recovery of course. In her own way. She knew that too.

'You're a stubborn bugger', she smiled gently. 'But if you ever change your mind and need to . . .'

'I know Beatrice. You're a dear, good friend. Let's get blinding drunk together sometime soon. In the meantime . . . what about Florence Nightingale?'

'There's a phone call for you Beatrice', Mrs Emsworth called across the issue desk.

Bea could see Mr Parkinson bristle indignantly. He objected to any form of communication above a whisper that disturbed the silence of the soundless library of his dreams.

'I'll leave you to it', Bea grinned. 'This could be news of my liberation.'

'How do you mean?' Harriet was intrigued.

'First prize in the staff raffle. A one way ticket for two to Australia. You could come with me if it wasn't for Maisie.'

In fact the phone call was from a hesitant and softly spoken Beatrice Trent, from a noisy phone box on campus at the University of Bath.

'I wanted to hear your voice', she said. 'See if you sounded legit.'

'I'm sorry to have alarmed you.' Bea replied. ' Did you mind me writing?'

'Your letter came at a funny time for me', the young woman said. 'I've been having these really strong feelings for months that I'd like to try and find my mother. Find out what really happened. Just so I know.'

'Do you know where she is', Bea asked gently.

'No I don't. She left when I was still quite young and I haven't seen or heard from her since.'

'But I know she sent you Christmas cards and birthday presents every year. The Post Mistress in your village remembers them being delivered.'

'Well I never received them. None of us did. That'll be my father. He's a pig if you want to know the truth.'

'Look, I know this may seem strange to you, Beatrice. And you must take lots of time to think about it. But I was really fond of your mother, and I dearly want to find her too. If you like, we could meet, you and I. And see if there's anything we can do about it together.'

'I don't know', the girl said. 'Maybe she has a new family. Maybe she wouldn't want to be reminded of us.'

'But maybe she would. She must have been pretty determined to keep sending you cards and letters long after she'd given up hope of you ever replying.'

'I would have replied. I didn't know. I loved my Mum. I hated it when she left.'

'But she doesn't know that. Or maybe she does. Either way – we could find out. Look, think about it. and phone me back in a few days if you want to meet me. I won't do anything else about it until I hear from you.'

'What's your first name?' the young woman said. 'I thought I heard them shout out Beatrice.'

'Yes. You did. I'm called Beatrice too. Quite a coincidence isn't it?'

'Is it? Look, I'll phone you back tomorrow when I've had a chance to think about it some more. Thanks for writing.'

'The Authority doesn't encourage private phone calls, Miss Hawksworth. I hope you are not letting your personal life intrude into your responsibilities.' Mr Parkinson seemed ever present on this frenetic Monday morning.

'If you have any complaints about my work Mr Parkinson, perhaps you could put them in writing. I'll take them up with the union.'

'Good for you', Harriet said when Bea told her. 'It's time you loosened your stays, to quote a Victorian metaphor'.

'More important', said Bea, 'What about young Beatrice? Obviously her father has kept all the information about Lotta well out of reach. She sounds so thoughtful and nice. Do you think she'll ring again?'

'I don't know. I hope so. Where will you meet her if she agrees to see you? Can I come?'

'I haven't thought about it. But of course you can come if you want to. If Beatrice doesn't mind.'

Bea was looking visibly excited and slightly agitated. 'Oh dear, Harriet. Can I cope with this? I'm too old for all this upheaval in my life. It's all your fault all of this. Poking me out of my rut with your crazy romantic notions.'

'You can't live on your memories forever Bea. You've still got half your life ahead of you girl.'

'The same could be said of you.'

'Me? I've got even longer. And I'm about to start making the most of it.'

Beatrice

By the end of the week Harriet had discovered, via the Post Mistress, that Lotta was writing to her children from somewhere in Lyme Regis. Young Beatrice had agreed to come for dinner in Woodleigh. And Helen was arriving by train from London at five o' clock.

On Friday Bea did something that was totally out of character. But symptomatic of a gleam, which the perceptive observer might have noticed had appeared in her grey green eyes, sometime around Wednesday morning.

Once Maisie was safely shepherded on to the mini

bus and heading for the day centre, she rang the library to say she was unwell and would be unable to come into work. No one doubted that she was sick, although it was unheard of for her to admit to illness in the past. Such was her dedication. When Harriet popped in, to confirm the arrangements for dinner, she was surprised to find her absent. No amount of phone calls could raise her at home and so she drove round to the house to make sure she was all right.

At the very moment that Harriet was knocking on her door in Woodleigh, Bea was happily ensconced beneath a hair dryer in Bournemouth, with a plastic hood over her head and tufts of pink prickles poking through specially constructed holes in the plastic. She was drinking coffee and leafing though fashion magazines to acquaint herself with what was current in the colour and cut of design. She had no wish to confront Helen and young Beatrice looking like a cross between Miss Marple and the retired Headmistress of a girls' boarding school. So it was time to take herself in hand.

As she watched the curious, sad face looking back at her from the salon mirror, she decided the haircut at least was an improvement. Jason had cut across the wave into a symmetrical bob that accentuated the shine and thickness of her hair. He'd peppered the strands of silver with peaks of deep magenta that caught the light as she turned her head. The result made her look at least ten years younger and she was well pleased.

The boutiques in Bournemouth were a revelation to Beatrice. She rarely bought clothes as a matter of choice and normally confined herself to the most subdued colours and voluminous styles in which to hide from the world. Today she bought jeans and bright silk shirts and fine cashmere sweaters in shades of dusky rose and jewelled aubergine and jade. She chose soft green leather boots, Chelsea style, and the kind of jacket that a lesbian of taste would select for a moonlight assignation. Even Maisie would be impressed, she decided, and risked £12.50 on a new woolly hat, in case the old lady could also be persuaded to dress herself up for the party the following evening.

Once liberated from the library, Bea decided to make the most of her day. She lazed through a rather expensive lunch at the Royal George Hotel and spent the afternoon in search of fresh crabs and wild mushrooms, starfruit and lychees. She bought a case of crisp white Bordeaux and six bottles of Brown Ale for Maisie. Hand made chocolates, white flowers and tall slender candles, the colour of Italian marble. She wanted to leave nothing to chance. Everything to be understated but perfect. She felt as though the party would mark the beginning of the re-invention of the rest of her life.

Harriet had guessed that Beatrice was skiving and decided not to worry. She spent the day in the garden, cutting back the debris of dry leaves and dead stalks to make way for spring bulbs, and watching where the hedgehogs had chosen to curl themselves away for the winter. Mr Smith was bounding about in reckless excitement, trying to coax her into his favourite game of chasing sticks. He piled offering upon offering at her feet, willing her with sharp furtive eyes, and a nagging insistent bark, to enter into the fun.

'I bet the old lady didn't do this all day', she said in exasperation. 'She wouldn't have the energy. Why don't you find a friend of your own persuasion to play with?'

At five she went to collect Helen from the station. She'd need to warn her about Mr Smith's bark. It was a case of being certainly much worse than his bite. He had hardly a tooth left in his head, and had taken to sucking his food through his gums, like an elderly judge deliberating on a verdict.

'Helen, my lovely girl, I'm so glad to see you.'

'How are you doing little sister? You're looking a hundred times better than when last I saw you.'

'That's not what Beatrice says. She says I'm shilpit.'

'What does that mean for goodness sake? It sounds like a disease.'

'It's an old phrase of Maisie's. It means pinched and sickly and undernourished, I think. But then Bea's an extremely healthy woman, on the whole.'

They walked towards the car and climbed in.

'How do you mean?'

'Well rumour has it at the library, that she's off work with some dreadful illness. But when I called round to see her earlier today, she was nowhere to be found. I think she's up to something. I hope she's up to no good!'

'I feel quite nervous about meeting Bea', Helen said. 'Tell me again what she's like'.

'You're the intimate correspondent to whom all has been revealed. You tell me. I thought all that pen pal stuff was just an excuse for getting it off with someone.'

'Harriet you've got a crude mind. Zenith is a very discreet association for women like us and not at all as you imagine.'

Harriet wasn't convinced. 'If you say so. Anyway, let me fill you in with the details. She's wildly beautiful, if you can sift your way through the shaggy-dog hairstyle and sensible tweeds in which she likes to disappear. She has the most compelling face, with sad grey eyes and pale olive skin. And she's big. Like a fine tree. But fearful and little inside. In odd moments you can see a free spirit struggling to escape but its as though she's wrapped herself in a grey woollen blanket for years and refused to come out. She's intense, as you said she would be. And spends a lot of time in her attic, communing with dead poets and woman novelists. She's suffering from lost love and sexual repression and could do with a bloody good dose of intemperate passion.'

'You sound a little in love with her yourself'. Helen watched her sister quizzically.

'Do I? That's not something that had occurred to me. But then I'm also fairly out of practice when it comes to romance. Bea is anxious about meeting you too, Helen. I don't know what you've said to each other in all those steamy letters.'

Helen laughed. 'I'm sure nothing that would shock you. Come on now. Take me home. I can't wait to see the cottage.'

Beatrice Trent arrived by bus in Woodleigh just after lunch on Saturday. She was small and dark and stocky like her father. But there the similarity stopped. Whereas he was moody and cautious to the point of inertia. Beatrice was idealistic and relentlessly optimistic. Whereas he was dull and gravely practical, Beatrice was a thinker. A vegan. A pacifist. A rebel. Whereas he was swift to disparage and condemn, Beatrice was open minded and the defender of a hundred lost causes. Bea wouldn't have recognised the young woman as Lotta's daughter by her appearance. But as she got to know her better, she could tell she had inherited much more than her mother's youthful enthusiasm.

Bea watched from the pavement as Beatrice got down from the bus at the village stop. She hadn't known what to expect, and probably another blond with twinkling blue eyes in her life would have been more than she could cope with at the moment.

And Bea looked nothing like Beatrice had expected either. She made a mental note not to make stereotyped assumptions about unmarried, small-town librarians, who lived at home with their aging mothers. The woman who came forward to shake her hand was tall and handsome, with spiky black hair that shimmered with splashes of pink and silver. She wore the kind of strong unusual colours the young woman would choose if she were not so self conscious and the kind of clothes she would like if she were not so small. They smiled at each other shyly. 'So' Beatrice said, 'You're Lotta's girl. I expect we have a lot to talk about.'

'I'll just warn you about my mother', Bea said as she opened the front door. 'She's totally dotty but extremely resilient. She talks rather at random, I'm afraid, the logic of which may surprise you with the odd truth, but most of which bears little relationship to anything of current significance. Here she comes now.'

Maisie came trotting into the hallway fully dressed in her winter coat and scarf, boots on the wrong feet, and new red woolly hat.

'This is Beatrice, Maisie. She's coming to have dinner with us this evening.'

Maisie looked confused. Two Beatrices in one day was

unusual by any standards. The young woman shook her hand warmly.

'You can call me something else if you like, if you get us mixed up'.

'This is Bea', Maisie said, pointing at her daughter. 'Who are you?'

'Don't worry about it', said Bea. 'She'll get used to you. She'll only remember your name if she decides she likes you. If she doesn't, you could be called Tutankhamun for all she'll care. We're not going out yet Maisie. Beatrice needs a cup of tea. Take your coat off poppet. Do you know where you put the fruit cake?'

'OK. No problem.' Maisie dropped her coat and scarf where she stood and went back into the sitting room to watch TV.

'She makes me laugh' said Bea.'That must be a line from one of her favourite television programmes "no problem". She says it all the time these days. Soon she'll be smoking cheroots and selling second hand cars.'

'Will you tell me about how you came to know my mother', Beatrice asked, as the two women sat in the kitchen drinking tea. 'I think she must have been very fond of you to give me your name.'

Bea hadn't imagined she would be so direct. She'd banked on a little small talk before she had to face the inevitable 'who are you' kind of question. But there was nothing to be gained from being obscure.'We were good friends when we were about the same age as you are now. We were pretty inseparable in those days. We worked together for a while. But then, for one reason and another , we lost touch'.

'I remember my mother singing to me as a child', Beatrice said. 'She was always singing. At least when my father wasn't around. They used to have the most terrible arguments. Me and the boys, we used to hide behind the bedroom door waiting for the shouting to die down. And then suddenly she was gone. My father said she was "a bad lot". I didn't know what he was talking about. I can't remember much more about it now. I think I must have blocked it out.'

The two women talked through the afternoon, trying to piece together what they knew of Lotta, to wonder what had become of her, and whether she would want them to search her out. As the time passed, the atmosphere lightened between them and they both became more relaxed.

'I hope that what I say doesn't offend you Beatrice, or upset you.'

The young woman smiled, conscious that Bea was struggling with her own embarrassment and shyness.

'You were lovers weren't you? You and Mum are gay.'

Bea looked surprised. Amazed at the perspicacity of the young. Or was it the street wisdom of a generation that had passed her by.

'How did you know?' she said.

'It's obvious really. She clearly loved you to give me your name. You clearly loved her to be still trying to find her after all these years. To be still crazy after all these years.'

Bea poured out a second cup of tea.

'All right' she said 'I'll tell you how it was. We were very young. And we were training to be nurses.' Outside the daylight began to fade and the walk in the Forest, that Bea had promised Maisie, became forgotten by all concerned.

'Why have you left it until now to try and find her?' Beatrice asked. 'It must be more than twenty years since you last saw her.'

'You could put it down to the mid-life crisis I suppose', Bea laughed sadly. 'But it's also got to do with Harriet. She's another long story. You'll meet her tonight so you can see for yourself. You may find this hard to believe but she's about the first real lesbian I've met since loving your mother. And, unlike me, she's open and easy about herself. She's made me face up to lots of things. Being lesbian for one. And laying ghosts for another. Do you mind her knowing about Lotta?'

'No I don't think so. I suppose, like Maisie, it depends on whether I like her or not.'

'I hope you don't mind me asking, Beatrice, but do you have any photographs of your mother from when you were small?'

'No father burned them all. He has always been poisonous about her. The mere mention of her name was enough to throw him into a rage that lasted for days. But I remember what she looked like. I can see her now in my mind's eye, chasing me through the meadows at the back of the farm, laughing with such gaiety and mischief. I loved her so much. I hated it when the boys were born.'

'It's just, maybe I should warn you. Perhaps it won't signify. But Harriet has a strong resemblance to Lotta. I noticed it as soon as I saw her. I thought a ghost had walked back into my life.'

'How strange', the young woman watched the sadness gather in Bea's thoughtful, serious eyes. 'And does Harriet know this too?'

'I haven't said. You're the only one I've told. I just wanted you to be prepared.'

'I wonder what she looks like now, my mother?'

'So do I'. Bea smiled. 'Like you, I see her in my dreams

exactly as I knew her then. I can't think of her as any different.'

'What happened to my lunch? You're always forgetting these days!'

'Maisie we had shepherd's pie at twelve o' clock. You had a second helping as usual. And ice cream. Which ended up all over your face. Did you remember the party tonight? I thought you might like to get dressed up a bit.'

'I might.' Maisie looked uncertain. 'Is Agnes coming?'

'No Sweetie, not tonight. But Harriet is and her sister Helen.'

'I like Harriet. That's no problem.'

By eight everything was ready. Maisie had been coaxed into a red woollen dress and was busily hiding the knives and forks that Bea had patiently arranged around the table at least three times already. She was distracted by the doorbell and trotted off to see who it could be. Bea had changed into shades of deep aubergine and old rose and was bracing herself with a stiff gin. Young Beatrice was blissfully unaware of the various levels of emotion operating in the social encounter into which she had stumbled. She was feeling innocently relaxed and curious. She heard the voices of greeting and Maisie being complemented on her new hat. She waited expectantly to see the young woman who would rekindle the image of her mother from all those years ago.

'Bea you look gorgeous, wonderful, stunning', Harriet was saying. 'So this is what your unexplained "illness" was all about! Bea, this is Helen.'

'So, we meet at last!' Helen was older and taller and rounder than Harriet, with the firm assurance of clothes

143

and a body and a hairstyle that have never been tempted to cultivate femininity. Of course she wore a waistcoat and sensible shoes. Bea knew she was going to like her.

'Harriet you're still looking weedy.' Bea said. And then, more audaciously than usual, 'I think I'll have to take you in hand.' The shadow of Lotta passed through her mind.

Helen watched in amusement as a faint blush stole across her sister's face. There wasn't much that escaped Helen's attention in the perilous game of lesbian romance.

'Come and meet young Beatrice' Bea said. 'I think you might like her.'

Maisie began to dish out the drinks with a rather reckless abandon as the other women were making their initial tentative greetings and assumptions. Harriet's glass arrived full to overflowing. Helen's with scarcely a drop of wine inside it.

'Don't take it personally', Bea laughed. 'She's excited. Maisie you haven't given Helen enough to drink. Do you want to try again?'Maisie sniffed in exasperation like a tired waitress at the banquet of life, who was totally unappreciated by her customers.

Beatrice saw in Harriet a woman of about thirty, looking pale and tired as if she was sleeping badly. But her manner was warm and attentive. She laughed a lot and teased Bea and Helen with a familiar and easy affection. She watched her help Maisie make better sense of the drinks and how quickly the old lady's irritation evaporated with Harriet's encouragement. But try as she might, she could not detect the slightest resemblance to her mother.

Warmed by the wine and the collective excitement in each other's company, the talk at dinner was all about women's writing and politics and history. With three lesbians, an old lady who couldn't remember whether she was or she wasn't, and a young radical, whose mother certainly was, there was much talk of romantic friendships and coming out and being gay and reinventing new ways of living. Maisie had no idea what was being talked about, but she caught the tone and enthusiasm of the argument going on around her. She nodded wisely as each woman made her contribution and occasionally burst into a little monologue herself, that was a jumble of words with no connection or significance, but which she issued with the same degree of conviction and intensity as everyone else. As she paused for breath, the others nodded in agreement until she too sat back in her seat, well pleased with her intervention.

'Can I ask you all' said Helen, feeling the time had come to be more specific 'to talk to each other, and to me and Maisie if you don't object, about what the search for Lotta means to each of you. You should know about each other's motives and anxieties. Have some clear idea about how you want to proceed. And what happens when you find out where she is as I'm sure you're going to.'

'Can't you just tell she's been on a counselling course?' laughed Harriet.

'I think its a good idea though' said Bea. 'Let's go and sit by the fire on some comfy chairs and I'll make a fresh pot of coffee.'

'Well I really don't want to interfere in anyone's privacy', Harriet began. 'But Bea and Lotta's story is so romantic and so poignant that I feel fascinated about how they could have come together so passionately as young women. Coming from no sense of being gay. Or from any sense of political commitment to women. Just from discovering each other. Falling wildly in love. Doing it, if you'll forgive my indelicacy Bea, against all odds. And then being forced apart. So that Bea felt she couldn't make a relationship with anyone else ever again. And Lotta, presumably, rushing into marriage as some kind of attempt to behave "normally".

'And then I see how my friend Bea has suffered as a consequence of her lost love, and has suppressed her own identity as a lesbian for years in some kind of dreadful self sacrificial atonement. I suppose in my arrogance, Bea, I want to liberate you from your attic, and your life of second hand experience through books, and from the old grey blanket you pull around your head when the world calls you out to play. I want you to love again in your own right. Maybe Lotta, maybe someone else. Certainly to love yourself. These are my reasons.'

Tears pricked against Bea's eyelids and seeped along her cheek. But she was smiling softly at Harriet's impassioned declaration of faith in romantic love and warmth on her behalf.

'If you only knew the half of it', she wanted to say but couldn't begin to.

Maisie patted her daughter's hand, still able to recognise the need for comfort without understanding the cause of her distress. 'No problem, Bea' she muttered. 'No problem.'

'How about you, young Beatrice?' Helen said. 'I think we should give Bea a moment or two to recover'.

'I feel really mixed up about the prospect of finding my mother.' Beatrice began hesitantly. 'In one way I feel she's completedy fucked up my life. Just when I loved her to distraction, and needed her, and expected her to always be there for me, she suddenly disappeared. With no warning. No explanation. No reason. My father never filled her place. I suppose he was in a state about it all as well. But he wouldn't talk to us about it. He just got angry. Kids at school said things. About my Mum leaving us. And about my Mum being queer. But I didn't know what they meant and my father wouldn't discuss it. All the time I was growing up. Being a teenager, all that stuff, I was surrounded by a family of men. I really missed having a mother I could talk to, and sort things out with. I felt angry with her all over again for getting out and not taking me with her. My brothers coped in different ways. Andrew, who's the youngest, used to wet the bed a lot and have dreadful tantrums for years. He still does sometimes. And now he's into computer games and spends all his time in his room zapping Martians. Hal is more like my father. Keeps his feelings, what few there are, on a tight rein. I'm sorry to say he joined the army as soon as left school. We don't get on. Andrew is the only one still at home and two years ago my father got married again. I don't get on with him either although I suppose I'm grateful to him for sticking by us.

'Recently, as I've started reading more about women's lives, and getting into feminism and politics I suppose, I've become more tolerant. Partly it's because I really like women now, and I want to make it all right with my mother before it's too late. And partly I know there must have been a good reason for her going, which made all other options seem impossible at the time.'

'Probably she thought she was doing the best for you. Leaving you in a secure and comfortable home.' Helen couldn't help intervening on Lotta's behalf. 'She probably had no money, no house to take you to, and knew that if it came to a court case, she'd be sure to lose custody of you anyway. Clearly she couldn't live in a straight marriage anymore. I can understand why she felt like that.'

'Yes I can understand that now', Beatrice said . 'At least I think I can. But what I don't know is how I'll feel if she's with someone else. Someone else who has children, maybe. I think I'll still feel jealous and angry.'

'How about you Bea?' Helen said gently. 'How will you feel if you find Lotta happily involved in another relationship?'

'Being realistic, I have to expect that she will be. Most people are in some way or other. And I don't want to think of her as being lonely or unhappy. Or wasting her life, like me. I suppose the honest answer is "I don't know". She might be a very different woman to the one I knew and fell in love with. I'm sure I am. At the very least, I'd like to think that we could make it all right with each other. Reassure each other that it all meant something special. Salvage a friendship possibly. Beyond that I don't know. I'm scared stiff.'

Now Harriet looked on the point of crying. She was feeling very tender towards Bea, very precarious about Maggie. Bea so honourable, Maggie so deceitful. But it's not always the good who gets the girl. Partly she knew that if Maggie were to press really hard, she'd give her another chance. And all of her knew she'd be a fool to try. Bea deserved to be adored. Maggie deserved to be shot. She felt too mixed up to make proper sense of it all.'

'What a weepy bunch we are', said Helen. 'I hope Lotta will be able to cope when you lot turn up on her doorstep.'

'Where are we going?' said Maisie. 'Do I need my boots?'

148

'We're going to bed Sugar Plum. Beatrice is staying the night but it's your turn first.'

'Come on Maisie, I'll help you up the stairs', said Harriet. 'You look tired out.'

'It's late for me Harriet', Maisie said with a rare clarity. 'But I've enjoyed myself with all you jolly girls.'

'You try and tell me your mother isn't a dyke Bea, and I won't believe you', Harriet laughed, as she helped Maisie off to bed.

Lotta

There's a stretch of beach along the coast where the sand is white, darkening to grey. The sea, deep crystal, flecked with spume, where the waves crash against the intransigence of the ragged cliffs. You can find rocks the size of boulders tossed from the mountains in more turbulent times, abandoned by centuries preoccupied with their own mortality.

Each spring the woman came to steal the rocks, as she had watched Berber tribesmen pillage the forgotten temples of Carthage for useful ruins. She heaved them into the back of her van and carried them under cover of darkness to her cottage by the cob. There she turned the rocks into memories of her life.

The woman's hair fell in tight curls to her shoulders, held back from her face by a lightly knotted scarf, the colour of her eyes. Her fingers held the the rock that was the child, its tiny head against her breast. She could feel the wrinkles, the fragile forehead, touch where the threads of pulsing veins struggled to concentrate. Feel the suck of greedy soft lips on her hard brown nipple. She took the chisel and mallet to sharpen where the eyes gazed in timeless wisdom into hers. The ancient rock stolen from the beach had become the child prised screaming from her breast in anger and confusion.

Sometimes she used clay instead of stone, pressing the points and folds of hip and belly into ridge and roundness, into hollow and smoothness against the light frame she had made. Feeling through her fingers where she too had rubbed and scratched and burrowed into flesh, remaking in her sculpture the sensations of a woman's body arched in passion.

'I am beautiful,' her lover said. 'You have made me like a mountain in a wild country.'

The woman laughed. 'Now I want to make love to your back and stretch myself upon you like a grey seal on an ancient rock.'

In the summer the woman worked on her boat, taking tourists to fish for mackerel in the Bay. Or along the rocky shoreline to Seal Island and Fossil Beach. Her pale skin turned brown in the sun, her strong arms dusted with a scatter of freckles. The woman wore heavy Indian jewellery, roughly worked in silver, with amber and lapis stone. Bright woven shirts and loose cotton trousers. By evening, when the tide was out, and the red, wooden hull of the boat lay sleeping by the harbour wall, she walked back along the cob to the cottage by the cliff. She smelled of the sea.

'I can taste the salt sea on your skin', her lover said. 'And now that you are truly mine, tell me of your life before we met.'

The woman cried. Her tears welling up against her eyes like a mountain spring breaking through a jagged tare in the hillside, from somewhere deep inside the earth. Her lover rocked her until the sobbing ebbed away and she drifted into sleep.

In the winter, when she wasn't working in her studio with the rocks, the woman was making good her boat. Replacing timber that was rotting and painting fresh patterns into the wooden deck. Sometimes she crewed for fishermen. Sometimes she walked the cliff face on her own, to where the echo of the gulls screeched against the empty sky.

'You look as though your mind is in another place', her lover said. 'Is something wrong?'

The woman held her close. 'A feeling I can't quite explain', she said. 'A longing in my spirit struggling to surface. An edge to my awareness. I feel I'm looking round each corner, over my shoulder, into the distance. Waiting for something to happen. Someone to touch me.'

'Are you restless? Do you want to leave?' her lover said.

'No Sweetheart. I'm through with running. It isn't that. It's just the past reaching into my heart, pounding in my brain. There's things I've left undone that need to be resolved.'

Her lover brought logs for the fire and a jug of wine.

'Tell me what you're feeling.'

They pulled the deep crimson, velvet curtains closed against the night and sat, legs entwined, intent and careful in the firelight.

'When I left my children', the woman said 'I thought I had no choice. I felt such hatred for myself. As though some deficit of mine, some feeling I couldn't control, had damaged my capacity to cope, my ability to live like everyone else. I felt such passion, such energy, such need. But none of it satisfied within the narrow confines of my life. At home I loved my children. My daughter like a second self. My boys so innocent and fragile and demanding. But I felt trapped, nailed down, my spirit bound and gagged and breaking. I thought I was going mad. I believed I was bad. I knew I couldn't stay. I thought their lives would be safer without me. For years I lived with those feelings, carried the self hatred into all my efforts to escape. I drank too much. Gave way to lust. Hated the women I fucked. Hated myself most of all.'

'What made the difference?' Her lover stroked gentle fingers along the curve of her back, easing the tight knot that had coiled around the muscle in her shoulder like a snake.

'Travel. Feminism. Sculpture. I began to discover reasons for my longing. Answers to my questions. Others who felt the same. I stopped feeling ashamed. Learned gradually to think better of myself. And then coming to live here. Loving you. Buying the boat. Walking by the sea. I've found some peace and I am almost whole.'

'So what is it now that troubles you after all this time?'

'I know it's inexplicable. I feel a strange strong surge of energy around me. Somehow I think they're looking for me.'

'But who Sweetheart?'

'I don't know exactly. Voices from the past. Maybe it's guilt for what I've done. Maybe it's strength because of what I've become. I need to make my peace.'

'Do you want some help?'

'I think I have to do it on my own. But I want you to love me. And I want you to understand. Even though I don't fully understand it myself.'

'Come lie with me' her lover said. 'And I'll stroke you till you sleep.'

Beatrice

'She's out!' Maisie slammed down the phone and covered it with a cushion. Bea was in the garden clearing the dead stalks and leaves from the winter cabbage patch to make room for spring greens. Beneath the apple tree, bright sharp spears of crocus and snowdrop were piercing the cold wet soil with shoots of survival and renewal. She was feeling restless and on edge, digging with exaggerated vigour to create distraction.

Three times she moved towards the phone. Three times the ringing stopped in seconds. She guessed the line was faulty. Peering round the kitchen door, Beatrice could see that Maisie was distressed.

'You OK old girl? Did I hear the telephone?'

'Trouble makers!' Maisie screeched, shaking her bony fists against her thin breasts.

Bea kicked off her wellingtons and gathered the old lady into her arms, soothing her as if a child. Stroking her wispy hair and rigid shoulders until the tension slackened and the pounding in her brain began to lighten.

'It's all right my Angel. No need to be upset. Tell why you're frightened.'

'Ringing. Always ringing!' Maisie wept clutching at her temples. 'Bad voices, Bea. Causing trouble in my head.'

Bea rocked her gently. Held her tightly until the sobbing ceased.

'Do you want to come and see the snowdrops Maisie? Some fresh air will do you good and I'd appreciate your company whilst I'm working.'

Maisie looked defeated. Then she opened the drawer in the kitchen table with renewed determination. She swept in the associated cutlery, place mats and napkins, and a half eaten bowl of Cherrios, and slammed it shut. A gesture of frustration more than anger. A need for order and control.

'Come on old girl. Let's get your coat and wellies. Come and tell me what you think about the snowdrops.'

At the other end of the line young Beatrice also struggled with frustration.'It's Maisie. She keeps hanging up the phone before I get chance to explain. We'll have to wait until she's gone to bed and try later.'

Lotta looked mightily relieved.

'Maybe it's for the best, sweetheart. It's taken me the

best part of half my lifetime to find you again. I don't think I can cope with Bea as well. Not both of you in the same day.'

Lotta smiled. 'Just give me a little while to catch my breath.'

Next morning Maisie went off to the centre in good spirits and Bea arrived at the library in good time. Mr Parkinson was taking a week's holiday and had left a list of instructions to occupy the underlings whilst he was gone.

A cursory glance at the first couple of paragraphs was enough to persuade Beatrice to hurl it in the bin.

'Miss Hawksworth. Please ensure that during my absence large print is reclassified into Thrillers, Biography and Romance and re-arranged into alphabetical order. Tell Mrs Emsworth to dust Gardening and Antiques, front and back, and tell Mrs Spencer to make a record in triplicate of overdue fines for my inspection when I return. You may have noticed that on Friday last, Miss Taylor was wearing jeans. I can only account for this aberration on her part by the unfortunate example set by yourself earlier in the week. It is my duty to remind you, as an employee of the Authority, and in a position of service to the general public, it is vital that proper professional standards are maintained at all times. Not least in the matter of appropriate dress and personal conduct. I am bound to say that I do not find your "new image" conducive to the position of Assistant Chief Librarian and trust that, on my return, you will have taken steps to return to normal . . .'

'Prat!' Bea muttered angrily with an exasperation loud enough to engage the attention of her fellow workers, who now waited with amused curiosity to see what would happen next.

'Right' said Bea. 'We have a week to transform this place and we might as well start now. Trudy, can you ring up the secretary of the Workers' Education Association and say the Chief Librarian has changed his mind. Say they can have the free use of our Reading Room on Thursdays for their Women's Studies discussion group. And Marjorie, just to make them feel at home, get rid of all that junk on military history from the display table and make us something splendid in green and purple to advertise International Women's Day. Julie, can you clear off all the ledges and polish up the window sills? The smell of old newspapers and fusty leaflets and empty collecting boxes for the Round Table is beyond my endurance any longer. When you're finished, you can take some money out of petty cash and fill the place with flowers.'

By the time Harriet arrived to return her books on Wednesday, she hardly recognised the library. The first thing she noticed was the noise. Not exactly mayhem, but laughter and the buzz of gossip. The playgroup were in the children's section painting pictures of Maisie who was sitting unusually still and wearing her tennis visor. Posters of women writers and performers had replaced the usual exhortations to attend church bazaars and VD clinics and the Reading and Reference Rooms were a profusion of pot pourri and white chrysanthemums. Julie was wearing a tartan mini skirt with green Doc Martens and a breezy Mrs Emsworth was pointing her next door neighbour in the general direction of Jane Rule and Maureen Duffy.

'Bea you look stunning', Harriet said. 'But don't you think the white linen shirt and black waistcoat is a little understated?'

'Jumble sale in the Masonic', Bea laughed, '75p the lot.'

Later in the Magnolia Cafe Harriet was full of curiosity. For once it was Beatrice who was late and Harriet who watched the door neurotically as customers drifted idly in and out. The Cafe was unusually quiet. Ralph was making shortbread in a desultory fashion. Gertrude Lawrence was singing 'Mad About the Boy' and Jack was nowhere to be seen.

'He's renegotiating his relationship somewhere south of Sienna', Ralph complained moodily. 'I should give him the bloody sack.'

'I thought Jack owned the business' Harriet said in genuine surprise.

'That's what everybody thinks. It's just that he likes the limelight. The glitz and glamour of cafe society in the thirties. The chance to be Noel Coward. Too bad it's only Winslow High Street and most of our clients are vegetarians.'

'Can I buy you a drink Ralph? You look thoroughly pissed off.' Harriet tried to lighten the exchange in the only way she knew how.

'It's ok Harry. I'm just being jealous and miserable. Next time around I'll confine myself to one trick at a time'.

'How are things at home?'

'Bloody awful. Just as you'd expect really. So much for the brave new world. We all might as well be married for the amount of difference a Gay makes.' He smiled ruefully.

Harriet didn't want to be hearing this analysis. It reminded her of Maggie, and the tasteless way she sometimes, for a joke, introduced her as 'the wife'. Harriet was getting impatient. It really wasn't like Beatrice to be late.

'You mean to say she's turned up of her own accord in Bath! But that's amazing! Beatrice, for goodness sake, tell me how it happened!'

'Well . . . Young Beatrice was in her room struggling with an essay on Katherine Mansfield . . .'

'For goodness sake Beatrice! Get to the point will you?'

Beatrice took a deep breath.

'Beatrice rang me last night about ten o clock. She was incredibly manic and, as you might expect, quite high on contradictory emotions. It seems that Lotta simply turned up on her doorstep. On Sunday, out of the blue. She had also rung the Post Mistress in a state of urgency about contacting her children, to discover, as we did, that Beatrice was in Bath and I was looking for her too. She's living in Lyme Regis, as we suspected, with a fishing boat and a woman called Joanna'.

Harriet could feel the anticipation sting her eyes. She held on to Bea's hands with total attention as the details of the story tumbled out.

'Beatrice says she's very beautiful and that you'll be

relieved to know she doesn't vote conservative or eat dead animals.'

Harriet squeezed Bea's hands as she saw the mixture of doubt and relief steal across her friend's face. Bea also looked like she might cry. The bravado had seeped from her shoulders as her thoughts slid back through half a lifetime of regret.

'There's enough weeping in this place already, without you two starting.' Ralph pushed two more cups of cappuccino along the counter beside them. 'No wonder the customers can't get out fast enough. It must feel like a sleepless night with a Russian novel. All we need is for the cat to collapse and I'll cut my throat.'

Beatrice and Harriet smiled weakly. It felt impossible in the circumstances to explain.

'You're a good sort Ralph' Harriet said sincerely. 'Too good to waste your sweetness on the desert air'.

He nodded. 'You're right, as usual, Harriet. It's not in my nature to be depressed for long. I'll sack the bugger and advertise in London for another. There must be more at home like you, in search of country air and a little peace and quiet out of the city.'

'Not quite like me, I imagine.' Harriet was laughing now. 'And don't offer him anything you can't deliver! Whatever else you might choose to say about this place, peaceful is not the adjective that springs immediately to mind.'

'Harriet I need to ask you a favour'. Bea was looking serious. 'It's not an easy thing for me to say and you must refuse at once if I'm intruding on your privacy in any way.'

Harriet was looking tired and not exactly recovered from her ordeal over Maggie. Bea knew she had to speak to Lotta.

'I've got a few days leave which I could take next week.'

'To visit Dorset? Does Lotta want to see you?'

'Beatrice says yes. And I think the time has come, don't you?'

Harriet nodded.

'But it's Maisie', Bea said. 'I wondered whether you'd mind . . .'

'Of course. She can stay with me. But will she agree to come?'

'Well you know what she's like. And you'll have to put up with the disappearance of anything you might leave lying about. But she likes you and Mr Smith. I don't really want to involve my sister in this unless I have to. It's a lot to ask, Harry. Say no if it feels too much.'

'To be honest Bea, I'll be glad of the company and the responsibility for a while. Too much introspection can become extremely wearing. Not to mention boring. Don't worry about Maisie and me. We'll be fine. Take as long as you need. I hope things turn out as you want them to be.'

Beatrice and Lotta

How did she want things to be? Bea thought she knew the answer, but the next part of the route seemed like a wild leap of faith towards a destination that was largely unknown.

It was a bright day as Beatrice drove across the moor and out of the Forest towards Lyme Regis. An early frost tipped the trees with ice. A fine mist crept along the ridge where the ponies, in their winter coats, followed each other in single file to the shelter of a hollow. The sun was bright like lemon sherbet. The crescent moon still a faded curl against the early morning sky. A thin layer of ice crusted the pond, cracked now into gashes of watery light where a swerve of mallard had slipped down from the bank to drink. Among the reeds swans slid in and out of the shallows, stretching an occasional wing to preen a careless feather.

As her car sped towards Dorset, the colours and the contours changed. The jagged heather and rough brown moorland grew softer and became more expansive. Gentle slopes of green, rounded against mellow valleys were shadowed by a shifting sky. Sheep bundled into winter coats grazed peacefully along the curve of wide and generous fields. Their boundaries etched in order with rows of hawthorn and pussy willow just breaking into bud.

The hamlet cottages and careful farms crouched in shades of cream and golden stone, reliable and sound. Flanked to the rear by ancient cliffs and beyond by the swell of blue black waves leading to another shore.

The journey provided Beatrice with the space for reflection and the opportunity for uncertainty. Occasionally she faltered. The consternation in her heart surfacing to counsel caution. What if Lotta had changed? Had ceased to place any significance on their early passion? Had become casual or insensitive about its meaning? She told herself to be prepared for disappointment. It was unlikely, after so long a time, that she would understand the persistence of Bea's feelings.

After all, what was the alternative? Did she really want to find a pathetic recluse, not unlike herself? A manic depressive? Hardly! She knew from Beatrice that there was someone else. A woman called Joanna. And possibly others. Of course Beatrice knew she should be pleased. She had no right to be jealous. Everything would be just as she expected. Over and done with.

And yet . . .

Beatrice had also said that Lotta wanted to make contact. That she too was full of memories and aware of possibilities. A woman of strong passions and deep emotions. Still crazy after all these years . . .

As Bea drew closer to the coastline, she could see the shops and houses of Lyme Regis in the middle distance, huddled beneath white limestone cliffs and thrown up against the sea on a grey shoulder of beach. She stopped the car and got out to taste the chill sunshine and draw the smell of sea salt into her lungs. Lotta was almost within reach now. Both half a lifetime and a few minutes away. She saw her on the bridge at Malham, laughing at the camera. She saw her crying from the carriage window as she was pulled away in tears by her angry father. She saw her this morning at the cottage door, standing beside Maisie and waving as Bea's car disappeared from view . . . The confusion startled her. Wrenching her from the sepia images of the past into a much more complicated present.

'No that was Harriet', she said aloud. 'This morning, that was Harriet.'

Beatrice saw her first. She was working on her boat, sanding a rough edge on the keel, stroking the mellow grain against the tips of her fingers to test the smoothness of her labour. The day was now bright and wayward. The sky veiled in whiskers of frail cloud that usually preceded rain. The uncertainty of storms at sea had pulled the gulls towards the land, where they wheeled and screeched around the cob, hungry and in pursuit of food. A few fishermen tidied and mended their nets on boats that dipped and rocked against the harbour wall.

She watched Lotta for some moments unobserved. Measuring the ease with which she steadied the sander, the care with which she assessed the smoothness of the wood against her skin. The focus of her concentration.

After a while Lotta turned, suddenly conscious of being studied. Standing to straighten the stiffness in her shoulders and to brush the dust from her faded red breeches. She was wrapped in layers of multi coloured sweaters against the chill breeze, like an onion wrapped in folds of secrecy. Her long curly hair tied back at the neck with a crimson scarf from India or Tibet.

She jumped from the boat on to the firm sweep of the cob where Bea hesitated nervously before moving to take hold of her outstretched hands. They looked at each other gently, without speaking for a while, arms extended, eyes searching for signs of recognition.

'My dearest friend' Lotta spoke first. 'You can't believe how good it is to see you again.'

She smiled tenderly as tears seeped from the corners of Bea's tightly shut eyes. Lotta reached to brush them away, with an intimacy that slid back across the years quite naturally.

'Would you like to sit in my boat?'

Bea nodded, still unable to speak.

'You look older', Lotta laughed, studying her face and watching where the brow creased into lines of concentration or sadness. 'And proud and enigmatic in your long black coat. Do you know about this place and *The French Lieutenant's Woman?*'

Bea smiled.

'Yes, I'm a librarian. I know the connection. Did you

mind me setting out to find you, Lotta? I've spent so much of my life absorbed with you. I needed to be free.'

'Free of me, do you mean?'

'Free of making you into my obsession. And of living in the past.'

'We were so very, very young', Lotta reflected sadly.'The victims of a kind of innocence. And such outrageous cruelty.'

'It was other people's ignorance and phobias, I suppose. Those were never the enlightened times they were supposed to be. Things would be different now, don't you think?'

'I'm not sure', Lotta said. 'For young women like my daughter, maybe. But choosing to be a lesbian still confronts a lot of bigotry and vested interests'.

'I loved you without any sense of confrontation', Bea said.

'Me too', Lotta smiled. 'It had a lot to do with lust and energy as I recall. And passionate friendship.'

'It's hard to explain. For years I simply missed you, as though my heart had shrunk and part of me had died.' Bea chose her words with care, in order to make Lotta understand. 'And although I tried, I couldn't let you go. Until you and my memories became the only relationship I could contemplate. I still talked to you in my head and made love to you in my fantasies.'

Now it was Lotta's turn to wipe her eyes. Eyes that, despite the sights they had seen, had rarely been allowed to cry. When she had regained her sense of calm she said, 'Would you like to walk with me a while? Before I take you home. We can walk along the headland to the next bay. It's a little uneven along the edge, but on a clear day, like today, you can sometimes see grey seal and cormorant.'

In places the track was just wide enough to walk together. In others they took turns to walk behind. Giving each the chance to collect confusing feelings and to savour the excitement of renewal.

'You didn't answer my question', Bea persisted. 'About making contact with Beatrice and coming here to find you. Do you mind?'

'When I knew at first, I felt afraid. Feelings I had tried to bury years ago came flooding back to shatter my defences. I had persuaded myself that you were history. A very important, but finished, moment in my life. The prospect of seeing you has disturbed me all over again.'

Bea couldn't imagine herself as one with the power to disturb anybody,'It's strong language, the language of disturbance', she said.

'These are strong emotions, Bea. Betrayal, obsession, jealousy, loss. The kind of emotions that cause people to kill themselves. To murder others.'

'Did you feel betrayed?', Bea said.

'Yes. I suppose I did. I loved you so much. I thought you should have been stronger. You should have been angry and defiant. Rode up on your white steed to rescue me.' She smiled now at her allusions to manliness and chivalry. 'I felt you didn't really care enough. Which, on top of being depicted as depraved by all around me, sent me hurtling into self hatred and matrimony with alarming consequences.'

'You should have told me', Bea looked distraught.

'You should have known', Lotta said.

It seemed possible to walk in silence for a while. Considering the possibilities. Searching for the words to

168

ask those private and important questions that had lain in limbo for so long.

'Have you been happy in your life?', Bea asked with tentative curiosity.

Lotta shrugged. 'When my children were small for a while. And more recently, since I moved here. Not often in between.'

'Has it been hard for you?' she persisted.

'I've sailed pretty close to the edge for a lot of the time. In ways I don't like to dwell upon. A shrink, presented with my life, would have a field day'. She smiled, trying to lighten the exchange. 'But as you can see, I pride myself on being a survivor.'

Beatrice nodded thoughtfully. 'You look "lived in", as I should have anticipated but not as I expected. You look tougher, too. And quite romantic in a way I hadn't bargained for.'

Lotta watched the sea intently, lost in some kind of guilty struggle with the past. Caught like a rainbow between earth and sky. She turned back towards the town.

'And what about you, my Darling? Tell me how you would describe your life. Now. From this vantage point. On the crest of this strange and significant day?'

Bea thought for a moment, concerned to be precise. 'I have picked away at life, Lotta. And stood back and watched it bleed and almost die. I think it's time to anticipate the future and stop living in the past.'

Lotta could tell that for someone like Bea, this gigantic leap of consciousness had come as something of a revelation. And should be treated with the utmost respect. She took her arm with familiar fondness.

'Let's hurry now', she said, 'The light is fading and I

want you to drink some wine and meet my women before you go.'

They walked back towards the cottage on the cob.

'Have you had other lovers', Lotta said, stopping to turn and face Bea, unsure about how she would feel.

Bea reached out her hand to brush a stray coil of hair from Lotta's eyes as though twenty years of abstinence were nothing. As though their intimacy had never floundered. 'No. Not so's you'd notice. Not yet anyway.'

Lotta caught Bea's hand and turned the palm towards her lips, kissing where the lines of life and love and fortune configured in a complex web of possibilities.

'I'm glad you've come back into my life at last', she said.

Bea smiled. 'I don't think you ever left mine.'

They walked arm in arm towards the cottage. The tall dark woman in black. The pirate with her yellow curls and rainbow colours.

'Now you must meet my women. Did you know that I creep out at dead of night and steal rocks?'

Bea looked puzzled.

'I'll show you', Lotta laughed. 'Through this door here.'

At the back of the cottage was a conservatory of sorts built in Victorian times to trap the sun and shelter vines and delicate palms. Now it was Lotta's workshop.

'This is the piece I'm working on at the moment', she said. 'The rock came from the island. Look, it has a strange blue line running through the grain. It catches the light against the seam. Here will be her breast and here the woman's shoulder.'

All around the workshop were Lotta's women – naked and asleep, arched in orgasm, thoughtful and perplexed, bold and demanding. Some curled round lovers. Some fiercely, independently their own.

'Do you exhibit them? or sell them?' Beatrice asked. 'They're magnificent, Lotta.'

'Some I sell. Mostly I can't bear to let them go. Sometimes I do children, like these'. She showed Bea fragile heads, their eyes alive with wonder. 'These are quite popular. less challenging, I suppose. They pay the rent. I feel odd about selling the women. They're erotic, I know. I don't want them in the hands of grubby minded men.'

'You could build up a lesbian market in London', Bea said. 'The word would soon get about.'

'I know. I know. Sometime, maybe I'll let them go.'

Bea could see that neither affluence nor reputation had occurred to Lotta. She touched the warm ripe shapes of breast and bum and belly with careful longing, the rock cool against her skin.

'Look here', Lotta said. 'She was my first. What do you think?'

The head was of a woman turned in anguish, her mouth open in a silent terrified scream, her eyes ablaze with horror.

'Self portrait circa 1968', said Lotta. 'I've let her have more fun as the years have gone by.'

Tears stung Bea's eyes and ran along the softness of her cheeks.She took Lotta in her arms and kissed her where her eyes were also wet with crying.

'You must forgive me now', she said, 'and let me love you in a new way.'

171

'As I get older', Lotta said, 'I think that friendship is probably the most important passion. Because it leaves you free to be yourself. It allows you to care passionately. But without the constraint of possession. I would dearly love you to say now that you will be my friend.'

Bea nodded, wiping the last of the tears from her cheeks.

'That's just what I hoped you would say', she said with determination and relief.

Beatrice and Harriet

Beatrice took some time out, to recover herself, before returning to the Forest. Maisie arrived back from holiday with rosy cheeks, a bunch of hazel catkins and a passion for Mr Smith that threatened to replace 'Neighbours' as the focus of her most immediate affection.

Next morning, when she was safely at the day centre, Beatrice set out with a basketful of daffodils and a bottle of champagne to visit Harriet.

'I could have said that I just happened to be passing, but it would be untrue. I wanted to see you.'

Harriet was looking curious. And a little shy. Bea was feeling ten feet tall. And well in charge of her intentions.

She held on to Harriet's eyes with the kind of fresh boldness that caused Harriet to smile nervously and look away.

'You seem immensely pleased with yourself', she said briskly. 'I take it you had a good time?'

Bea watched her as though she was looking at her for the first time.

'I've never mentioned the blush that steals across your throat when your heart is beating fast', she said. 'Or how the sunshine suits you.'

Harriet piled the daffodils into a jug of water from the well. Her heart was racing it was true. She could feel it thumping against her chest. She poured them both a glass of wine.

'A little early in the day but here's to you, Sweetheart'. She raised her glass in tribute. 'You look like the cat that got the cream. And I'm going to become extremely irritated with you if you don't stop staring at me like that and tell me what's happened. Or do I have to drag it out of you?'

'Do you know, I think my life has been given back to me.' Bea could hardly contain herself. 'What a miserable specimen I was when you first came and dug me out of my hole. I was dead from the neck down.'

'Oh, I wouldn't say that exactly.' Harriet was smiling. 'If you were an actress, you'd probably say you'd been resting.'

'Rotting more like. Thank you for rescuing me.'

'A pleasure. So what happened? Did you meet up with Lotta? What's she like?'

'Harriet, she's wonderful! She's so brilliant. She's sensitive. Clever. Strong. She can build boats and catch fish.

And she makes beautiful, erotic sculptures out of rock.
You'd really like her!'

Harriet was beginning to have her doubts.

'Was she pleased to see you?'

'She was, actually. She said she'd had some kind of
premonition that I'd come. She's had a hard life, you
know. Lots of pain. But she's a survivor, Harriet. I felt
like I'd known her all my life'.

'You have haven't you?'

'Well, not really. Not the way she is now. I was stuck
in some kind of time warp wasn't I? It's not really fair to
do that to someone. It'll be better now. We can love each
other for the women we really are. And not some faded
photographs.'

Harriet took another sip of champagne. She was feel-
ing small suddenly. And lonely. The cottage was a mess.
A reflection of her mood. She wished she'd had a haircut.
Worn her new blue shirt.

'I'm glad you liked each other.' Harriet hesitated.

'I've got you to thank for all of this, Harriet. Helping
me to find Lotta. I'd have never done it without you. Now
I feel that everything is possible.' Bea looked as though
she might bubble over and burst like the champagne
against her tongue.

'There was no problem with Maisie. She was fine'.
Harriet tried to sound enthusiastic but she was feeling
increasingly depressed.

'I meant to thank you. For having her, I mean. She
likes it here. She's in love with Mr Smith.' Bea was
laughing. 'And how have you been? It seems ages since
I've seen you. So much has happened to me. I feel like
I'm flying.'

'Oh, not a lot. I've been trying to write a bit .... but
without much inspiration.'

It was odd. Harriet would have given blood a few months ago to discover Bea in a mood like this. But now she felt confused. How could anyone resist her? She looked so proud and joyful. What an ending to a story. Lotta was indeed a lucky woman.

'I've been thinking. I might go back to London. I need to get a proper job.'

Beatrice was suddenly quiet.

'You're joking. You're not serious. But I thought you took the lease for another year at least.'

'What's the point, Bea? There's nothing for me to do here really. I could end up like you were. Dead in a hole.'

'Harriet this isn't like you.' Bea was in too good a mood to put up with this unnecessary fit of despair. 'I thought the time at Heather Hill had been a turning point for you too.'

'I'm sorry Bea to spoil your fun. It's unforgivable of me to be morbid when you're so happy. Let's have another drink. To you and to the future.'

'Harry, I think you might be getting slightly the wrong idea about all of this. I'm not about to disappear into the distance you know. Not unless you want me too. I came to thank you for helping me to find Lotta. But mostly for helping me to find myself. I feel I'm worth something at last. Worth loving, maybe.'

'Bea you're an angel! How could anyone not love you?' Harriet was now extremely serious. 'I'm sure Lotta does, for example.'

'I hope she does. I certainly love her. I always have and I always will. But in a different way. Like a very, very good friend whose life is tied up with mine in ways that feels like family. Do you know what I mean?'

Harriet wasn't sure. 'Maybe'.

'The other reason I came . . .' Beatrice took a deep

breath. She was blushing slightly but quite determined. 'Was to hold you ... like this ...'

She took Harriet's glass and placed it on the table by the door. Then she moved closer, taking her hand and raising it to her lips. Harriet moved into her arms as though it was the most natural movement in the world, encircling herself like a halo round the sun.

Their first kiss was just the merest brush of lips. Beatrice felt her body tremble and her heart plunge somewhere deep into her stomach. She could smell the Forest in Harriet's hair, like sunshine after rain. She watched where it fell in wayward curls across her face. Gently, deliberately Beatrice began smoothing back the strands, until she found her eyes again, and watched where her lips moved as though they wanted to be kissed. When Harriet raised her eyes to look at Bea, they were misty and bluer than robin's eggs. Their lips touched briefly for another second, each retreating in surprise as though a current flashed between them, charged with intensity.

Harriet was in some confusion at the sudden change of direction in their friendship. Her voice a little husky, her throat dry.

'So', she said softly, 'you decided to come out to play at last. No prize for guessing what game you have in mind.'

Bea rocked with laughter, suddenly delighted by the ridiculous notion of herself as someone 'up to mischief'. And then she smiled quizzically as she considered the consequences of what might happen next.

'I came to make love to you', she said. 'That is, of course, unless you still intend to take the next train back to London.'

Harriet moved swiftly into the urgency of Bea's arms

and kissed the tiny triangle of flesh that glistened where her fine woollen shirt opened to reveal pale olive skin and to conceal soft rounded breasts. She led her to the wooden stair that climbed towards her bedroom in the eaves.

'Why have I never told you that you look so lovely?' Harriet said. 'That I have longed to kiss the sadness from your eyes and make them smile again?'

'Tell me now', Beatrice whispered. But then she kissed her long and gently before another breath could come between them.

'I could only imagine how your lips would be', she said, 'How soft and moist. How sharp your teeth.'

'Come to bed', Harriet said. 'Or do you take perverse pleasure in procrastination?'

When Beatrice woke up she was alone. It was almost dark and she was lying beneath the hand embroidered spread of peacock feathers and lily flowers that was thrown across Harriet's bed. Somewhere in the distance an owl hooted and the wildness of the Forest prepared for sleep.

For a moment she was unsure about where she was. Whose bed? Which fantasy? Her muscles ached in places she'd forgotten that muscles existed. Getting out of bed and walking, felt like wading though treacle. A little smile of pleasure crept across her face as the delights of the day returned. They had drunk wine and made love; and told stories and made love; and laughed and made love for most of the afternoon. Something of a vindication for the doctrine of positive thinking and direct action, she conceded. Though not, alas, in ways that were likely to reassure Mr Parkinson.

Downstairs the fire was crackling in the grate and a bottle of red wine was open on the table beside three heavy crystal goblets. Delius was playing from the Albert Hall, courtesy of Radio Three. And the daffodils she had brought earlier in the day, as tight green buds beneath pale brown sheaths, had burst into a riotous array of yellow and white flowers. She smiled as she remembered Harriet's delight the very first time she brought flowers to her old lady's cottage by the moor.

Beside the open door Mr Smith was poised for action, like a ticket seller at a jumble sale, waiting for the punters to arrive. He wagged a scrappy tail in welcome as Beatrice descended, rather stiffly, down the wooden stairs. And confined himself to a half-hearted yelp of appreciation as she knelt to rub and scratch his scraggy head. His attention was focused on the sound of a car in the distance which had a familiar rattle. Especially as it turned the corner into the lane and clattered to a standstill at the garden gate.

The arrival of the yellow beetle acted like the spark that starts a riot. Mr Smith bounded along the path, barking and yelping and wagging his tale. Unsure whether to collect his pile of sticks now, or whether to throw himself at the car door until its passengers climbed out and agreed to play. Beatrice followed smiling. The slight frisson of anxiety that it would be Maggie in the car, coming to claim the third glass of wine, quickly evaporated as she saw the beaming and delighted face of Maisie, waving ecstatically at Mr Smith. Harriet jumped out of the driver's seat and ran into Bea's arms, hugging her as if she'd been away for weeks.

'First scent of passion and your sense of family

responsibility goes out the window', she teased. 'Good job you can count on me to act reliably.'

'God! You're absolutely right, Harriet. How on earth could I forget about Maisie after all this time?'

'Because you're crazy. And I imagine, although I may be wrong, that your mind is otherwise engaged because you have fallen head over heels in love with me!'

Meanwhile Maisie was banging impatiently on the window and Mr Smith was flinging himself against the car door.

'We'd better sort these two out', Beatrice laughed.

'Hello Sweetie, how are you?'

'Hiya Smithey', Maisie shouted, apparently oblivious to Bea's belated sense of guilt. 'Watch out, Bea. I'm getting out of this car. You've been up to no good again, I suppose ' She shook her head as if this was a common occurrence and shuffled past to throw Smithey a stick.'

'We stopped to collect fish and chips on the way home', Harriet said laughing. 'I thought you might like to stay for supper.'

Sometime later Beatrice recorded the evening in her diary, as she sat in the attic at home with the scent of Harriet's perfume and the touch of her fingers printed indelibly across her body and her mind.

'My first candlelight meal in more than twenty years', she wrote.

'Not on my own, but with my very beautiful and most wonderful new lover, Harriet. Somewhere in the distance Delius was playing in the Albert Hall and my mother Maisie got slightly tipsy drinking red wine out of a crystal goblet.'

Silver Moon Books

Publishers of Lesbian Romance, Detective and Thriller Novels

FLASHPOINT, KATHERINE V. FORREST
A contemporary novel in which Katherine V. Forrest brings together all the skill and passion that have made her the most popular lesbian author writing today.
(£6.99, 240pp, ISBN 1 872642 29 2).

DIVING DEEPER, eds KATHERINE V. FORREST and BARBARA GRIER
Silver Moon's second anthology of erotic lesbian short stories takes over where its predecessor *Diving Deep* left off.
(£6.99, 304pp, ISBN 1 872642 225).

UNDER MY SKIN, JAYE MAIMAN
Following on from the success of *I Left my Heart and Crazy for Loving,* this third book in award-winning Jaye Maiman's highly-charged mystery series is the best yet.
(£6.99, 285pp, 1SBN 1 872642 26 8).

DEAD CERTAIN, CLAIRE MCNAB
Faced with the exposure she has always feared, her integrity and objectivity questioned as never before, Detective Inspector Carol Ashton finds her professional and emotional life spinning out of control in this scorching thriller.
(£6.99, 206pp, ISBN 1 872642 28 4).

SILENT HEART, CLAIRE MCNAB
A moving and erotic love story from the author of the bestselling *Under the Southern Cross.*
(£6.99, 173pp, ISBN 1 872642 16 0).

A TIGER'S HEART, LAUREN WRIGHT DOUGLAS
A sizzling thriller from the author of bestsellers *Ninth Life* and *Chasing the Shadow* to keep you on the edge of your seat until its gripping final page.
(£6.99, 220pp, ISBN 1 872642 12 8).

DIVING DEEP, eds KATHERINE. V. FORREST and BARBARA GRIER
Silver Moon's first short story anthology brings together stories of love, desire, romance and passion.
(£6.99, 218pp, ISBN 1 872642 14 4).

UNDER THE SOUTHERN CROSS, CLAIRE McNAB
Claire McNab departs from her famous Detective Inspector Carol
Ashton series to bring her readers this passionate romance set
against the majestic landscape of Australia.
(£6.99, 192pp, ISBN 1 872642 17 9).

CRAZY FOR LOVING, JAYE MAIMAN
Romance and mystery with detective Robin Miller loose in New
York. Jaye Maiman at the top of her form in this sequel to the very
popular *I Left My Heart*.
(£6.99, 320pp, ISBN 1 872642 19 5).

PAPERBACK ROMANCE, KARIN KALLMAKER
Literary agent Alison, romantic novelist Carolyn, and the enigmatic
conductor Nicolas Frost – who is *certainly* not what he seems –
come together in this fast moving, erotic lesbian love story.
(£6.99, 256pp, ISBN 1 872642 13 6).

THE GARBAGE DUMP MURDERS, ROSE BEECHAM
A monster is on the loose – his victims a grisly jigsaw puzzle of
anonymous body parts left around the city. Set against him is
Amanda Valentine, a tough and unusual cop. Unpredictable, passionate and, as adversaries and lovers quickly learn, very much her
own woman.
(£6.99, 240pp, ISBN 1 872642 15 2).

LOVE, ZENA BETH, DIANE SALVATORE
The novel all lesbian America is talking about. The story of Joyce
Ecco's love affair with Zena Beth Frazer, world famous lesbian
author. Zena Beth is sexy, witty, outrageous and recovering from
her sensational love affair with sports superstar Helena Zoe. A passionate novel of love and jealousy which has the ring of truth.
(£6.99, 224pp, ISBN 1 872642 10 1).

CHASING THE SHADOW, LAUREN WRIGHT DOUGLAS
As the action builds to its nerve tearing climax Caitlin Reece must
face a moral dilemma which nearly costs her her life. A hard-hitting
and hugely entertaining thriller which packs a heart-stopping sting
in its tail.
(£6.99, 224pp, ISBN 1 872642 09 8).

COP OUT, CLAIRE McNAB
A bestseller from this very popular author. The story of the Darcy
family – a family at war – and the killer who menaces it. Can Carol
Ashton find the murderer before it is too late?
(£6.99, 191pp, ISBN 1 872642 08 X).

A THIRD STORY, CAROLE TAYLOR
A fine novel about the pain of hiding, and the joy of coming out told with great humour and compassion.
(£5.99, 133pp, ISBN 1 872642 07 1).

I LEFT MY HEART, JAYE MAIMAN
As she follows a trail of mystery from San Francisco down the coast travel writer and romantic novelist Robin Miller finds distraction with sexy and enigmatic Cathy. A fast paced and witty thriller from an exciting new talent.
(£6.99, 303pp, ISBN 1 872642 06 3).

NINTH LIFE, LAUREN WRIGHT DOUGLAS
Introducing Caitlin Reece, uncompromising, tough, a wisecracking lesbian detective who takes no nonsense from anyone.
(£5.99, 242pp, ISBN 1 872642 04 7).

BENEDICTION, DIANE SALVATORE
A wonderful story of growing up and coming out. Its progress through love, sexuality and friendship will awaken so many memories for us all.
(£5.99, 260pp, ISBN 1 872642 05 5).

DEATH DOWN UNDER, CLAIRE McNAB
Detective Inspector Carol Ashton returns in the most formidable, baffling, and important homicide case of her career.
(£5.99, 220pp, ISBN 1 872642 03 9).

CURIOUS WINE, KATHERINE V. FORREST
An unforgettable novel from bestseller Katherine V. Forrest. Breathtakingly candid in its romantic eroticism – a love story to cherish.
(£6.99, 160pp, ISBN 1 872642 02 0).

LESSONS IN MURDER, CLAIRE McNAB
A marvellous tale of jealousy, murder and romance featuring the stylish Inspector Carol Ashton.
(£5.99, 203pp, ISBN 1 872642 01 2).

AN EMERGENCE OF GREEN, KATHERINE V. FORREST
A frank and powerful love story set against the backdrop of Los Angeles, this passionate novel pulls no punches.
(£6.99, 270pp, ISBN 1 872642 00 4).

Silver Moon Books are available from all good bookshops. However, if you have difficulty obtaining our titles please write to Silver Moon Books, 68 Charing Cross Road, London WC2H 0BB

SILVER MOON BOOKS
LESBIAN PUBLISHING FOR THE 1990s
What the Press have said

"If you thought lesbian fiction was worthy but unskilled writing for an oppressed minority, move over darling. Today Silver Moon Books launch Friday Night Reads, a series of fun books for lesbians"

THE GUARDIAN

"Shine on Silver Moon"

THE OBSERVER

"...much welcomed new lesbian publishing house"

TIME OUT

"Silver Moon's first two books are indeed fun and erotic"

EVERYWOMAN

"Publishers with a mission to rescue lesbian readers across the nation from...tedium"

THE GUARDIAN

SILVER MOON BOOKS publish lesbian romance, detective and thriller stories. The accent is on FUN, our books are ideal for weekends at home or journeys away. So, when you want entertainment think of us first.